Praise for Melody Carlson's Christmas Novellas

"In this wholesome holiday standalone from Carlson, a woman finds community in unexpected places. This is perfect for fireside reading on a cold December night."

Publishers Weekly on *A Quilt for Christmas*

"I look forward to reading Melody Carlson's Christmas stories every year. She comes up with the most interesting adventures that involve family, have a splash of romance, and always get to the heart of the season."

Interviews & Reviews on *A Quilt for Christmas*

"The perfect book to get one in the Christmas mood. It is heartfelt, engaging, and romantic. Second chances, new beginnings, and hope are in full swing in this amazing read."

Urban Lit Magazine on *A Christmas in the Alps*

"*A Christmas in the Alps* is old-world charm with a sneaky romance drizzled in that leaves you wanting more!"

Romance Junkies on *A Christmas in the Alps*

"Romantics will swoon and feel they have enjoyed an evening or two with a simple romance. This is perfect for those wanting a quick feel-good holiday read."

Compass Book Ratings on *A Christmas in the Alps*

"A perfect book to curl up with by the fire and catch some cozy Christmas romance vibes."

Fresh Fiction on *The Christmas Swap*

"Carlson's latest Christmas romance is as light and sweet as a Hallmark movie."

Booklist on *The Christmas Swap*

A Royal Christmas

Books by Melody Carlson

Christmas at Harrington's

The Christmas Shoppe

The Joy of Christmas

The Treasure of Christmas

The Christmas Pony

A Simple Christmas Wish

The Christmas Cat

The Christmas Joy Ride

The Christmas Angel Project

The Christmas Blessing

A Christmas by the Sea

Christmas in Winter Hill

The Christmas Swap

A Christmas in the Alps

A Quilt for Christmas

A Royal Christmas

A Royal Christmas

A CHRISTMAS NOVELLA

MELODY CARLSON

Revell

a division of Baker Publishing Group
Grand Rapids, Michigan

© 2023 by Carlson Management Company

Published by Revell
a division of Baker Publishing Group
Grand Rapids, Michigan
www.revellbooks.com

Printed in the United States of America

Library of Congress Cataloging-in-Publication Data
Names: Carlson, Melody, author.
Title: A royal Christmas : a Christmas novella / Melody Carlson.
Description: Grand Rapids, Michigan : Revell, a division of Baker Publishing Group, [2023]
Identifiers: LCCN 2022050887 | ISBN 9780800742317 (cloth) | ISBN 9781493443451 (ebook)
Classification: LCC PS3553.A73257 R69 2023 | DDC 813/.54—dc23
LC record available at https://lccn.loc.gov/2022050887

Baker Publishing Group publications use paper produced from sustainable forestry practices and post-consumer waste whenever possible.

23   24   25   26   27   28   29   7   6   5   4   3   2   1

CHAPTER

One

After more than eight years of crafting "clever" custom beverages at Common Grounds Coffee, Adelaide Smith was ready to call it quits. Instead, she smiled stiffly at the pair of teen girls stepping up to the counter. "What can I get you?"

"I'll have a venti vanilla latte, nonfat milk, whipped cream, five Splendas with one Sugar In The Raw packet on the whipped cream," the first girl said.

Adelaide's brows arched. "Raw sugar on top?"

"You know, to make it crunchy." The girl pulled a card from her wallet.

"Uh, right." Adelaide maintained her poker face over the slightly schizophrenic order, then she turned to the second girl. "How about you?"

"I want a venti iced latte, with six ristretto shots, with breve, four pumps of vanilla, five pumps of caramel, and three Splenda. Poured not shaken."

Adelaide blinked. Were these girls for real or was she being filmed by some YouTube jokester? Glancing around, she saw no phone aimed her way, and both girls seemed genuine as they took turns running their cards with, of course, no tips. Then as she meticulously relayed the convoluted orders to her boss, Vicki, who broke into loud giggles, Adelaide noticed her best friend, Maya, frantically waving at her from outside the shop.

Was Maya behind this little gag? But Maya just pointed to her little electric car, parked in the fifteen-minute space, and then to her watch. The big clock behind the counter confirmed Adelaide's shift was indeed over. And knowing Maya would be eager for her coffee—the usual payment for Adelaide's ride home—and less eager to move her car or be ticketed, Adelaide started on Maya's usual venti mocha with skim milk. Now that was a sensible order.

"Can you believe this?" Vicki laughed as she sprinkled sugar on top of the whipped cream, then pointed to the five empty Splenda packets. "Go figure, huh?"

"I know." Now, instead of making her usual end-of-shift latte with whole milk, Adelaide filled a cup with hot water, then plunked in a peppermint tea bag.

"What, quitting coffee, are we?" Vicki frowned as she slid the second complicated order on the counter and called out the girls' names.

"Not permanently." Adelaide removed her apron. "But with only two days left here, I thought I should start weaning my-self."

Vicki shook her head. "I still can't believe you're really leav-ing us."

"I should've done it sooner, Vicks. Not because of you and Lance. But you know I should be in my externship by now." Adelaide reached for her parka. "Hopefully I'll secure some-thing before January."

"Well, you'll be missed around here." Vicki sighed as she put a lid on the mocha. "Not to mention we'll be shorthanded during the holidays."

"Sorry about that, but I warned Lance several weeks ago."

She tugged on her gloves. "You know how your husband lives in denial."

"Yeah, but you've given notice before without quitting. Good grief, Addie, you've been here longer than our espresso machine."

Adelaide laughed as she picked up the to-go cups. "One more good reason it's time for me to move on. See ya tomorrow, Vicks."

Barely out the door, Adelaide was greeted by Maya. "I'll take that." Maya retrieved the mocha before they both piled into Maya's pint-size car.

"Sorry to be so late." Adelaide sniffed her tea, wishing she'd gotten her usual latte instead. "Guess I was distracted." She explained about the last two crazy-making orders, and they both laughed. "I still can't believe Monday will be my last day there."

"We should do something to celebrate."

"I guess." Adelaide released a long sigh.

"Don't tell me you're sad about leaving."

"A little. The owners have been like a second family to me. Especially after Mom died. It's hard to let relationships like that go."

"You'll still be friends with Vicki and Lance." Maya pulled out into the slow-moving traffic.

"I suppose, but it's like the end of an era."

"Who knows, maybe you'll be representing them a year from now."

Adelaide stared at her friend with wide eyes. "Legally? What do you mean? You think they're getting sued?"

"No, of course not. But businesses need lawyers, don't they?"

"Yes, but I'm not going into corporate law." Adelaide sipped her tea, then grimaced. "Ugh."

"Huh?"

"This tea. Don't know what I was thinking." Adelaide let down the window and tossed out the hot fluid, careful not to hit Maya's car.

"That does it, Addie! I'm taking you out for dinner to celebrate the end of your coffee career. I'd suggest we wait for your last day, but I have PTA Monday night. Where do you want to go?"

"I don't know. I don't really feel like celebrating. Besides, it's Saturday. Any place good will be full."

Maya shook her head. "Why this Eeyore act? Is this about parting with Common Grounds or is something else going on? You're not usually such a buzzkill."

"I know. It's probably this time of year."

"Oh, yeah, I totally forgot your mom died in late November. I'm sorry."

"Thanks. It's probably more than just that. Forgive my little pity party, but I'm feeling bummed over how long it's taking to get through law school. I know younger attorneys with well-established practices, and here I am still slinging coffee and—"

"Don't be so hard on yourself. You got this far on your own. When you start practicing law, you can be super proud of your achievements. Nobody handed it to you on a silver platter."

"And I can say the same about you. You put yourself through college too. But unlike me, your tuition is paid off. I still have a pile of college debt and—"

"Yeah, but it's taken seven years, and I'll never make as much as you. I'm only a teacher and—"

"*Only?* You know how important teachers are, Maya! Haven't I told you how proud I am of you?"

Maya laughed. "Like a million times."

While bantering over which was better—to be loved by little children and get paid less or earn the big bucks and be despised by many—they drove around looking for a good dinner spot that wasn't overly packed until Maya finally admitted her car's battery was running low.

Adelaide pulled out her phone. "There's Robie's Barbecue down the street. I'll call in takeout and we can pig out on ribs in privacy. They just put in a new charging station down the street from my house. We can eat there while your car juices up."

"Now that sounds like a sensible plan."

"Just promise not to criticize the housekeeping or"—Adelaide paused to place their order.

"I never criticize your housekeeping," Maya said after Adelaide hung up. "I just criticize your house."

"It's not *my* house," Adelaide defended herself. "Only the second floor. And Mrs. Crabtree could charge me twice as much if she liked. Probably three times."

"Not once a potential tenant saw her seven cats. Or smelled them."

"She's down to six now," Adelaide said. "Sweet Pea died last week."

As they waited for their order, Maya continued to challenge Adelaide's preference of a landlady who preferred felines to paying higher rent. But as they drove the short distance to the hundred-year-old home Adelaide shared with Mrs. Crabtree, she felt confident the jury would side with her persuasive argument. She'd never get a whole second floor somewhere else for what she paid each month. Besides, she'd been with the old woman ever since her mom died.

"I have to give it to you, Maya," Adelaide said, "you've always been a good sport in our friendly debates. I guess you know how much I love a good argument."

"I've always known you'd make a good lawyer."

She smiled. "I think we've been agreeing to disagree ever since you told me *Finding Nemo* was better than *Shrek*," Adelaide pointed out. "Remember how we almost came to fisticuffs over it?"

"Yeah, in third grade." Maya laughed as she plugged her car into the charging station. They carried the food into the house, and Adelaide noticed Maya's nose wrinkle when she opened the door. Snatching her mail from the basket in the foyer, Adelaide called out a warm greeting to Mrs. Crabtree, then hurried up the creaky stairs. Admittedly, the aroma was stronger than usual tonight. At the top landing, she grabbed her can of lavender air freshener and gave the stairs and hallway a liberal spray before rushing into the room she used as her study and closing the door behind them.

"Whew, that was bad." Maya opened a bag of aromatic barbecued food and literally stuck her face into it, inhaling loudly.

"What a drama queen," Adelaide teased.

Maya emerged from the bag with a furrowed brow. "I don't see how you stand it, Addie. Seriously?"

"It doesn't smell bad in here, does it?"

Maya sniffed, then shrugged. "Just that usual musty old book odor that you seem to thrive on. You remind me of my grandpa."

"Maybe I should smoke a pipe too."

"That might help." While Maya unloaded dinner onto the wooden crate that served as a coffee table, Adelaide went to the cabinet she'd turned into her minikitchenette and got out two paper plates. Then, as Maya divvied out ribs, corn on the cob, mac and cheese, and coleslaw, she reminded Adelaide that she'd invited her to share her two-bedroom apartment more than once. "But you'd have to get rid of some of your junk." She gestured toward an overflowing bookshelf.

"I've spent years collecting these books," Adelaide said defensively as she sat down. "Not only are they a valuable investment but they're also good resources."

"Information I'm sure you could find online."

"But these books make me happy." Adelaide picked up a rib with one hand and used the other to thumb through her mail. She had several pieces of tree-wasting junk mail, as well as an odd-looking legal-size envelope. "Interesting." She turned it over.

"What's that?"

Adelaide studied the return address. "I've never seen any-thing like this. It says it's from the Principality of Montovia."

"Sounds made up. Probably a scam." Maya reached for an ear of corn.

"A scam from Montovia?"

"Where on earth *is* Montovia?"

"Montovia is a European country. I think it's near Austria or Hungary. But it's tiny. Even smaller than Liechtenstein."

"What's Liechtenstein?"

Adelaide's mouth dropped open. "Didn't you take *any* ge-ography in school?"

Maya made a face as she chomped into her corn.

Adelaide wiped her fingers on a napkin, then, using a clean plastic knife, slit open the sturdy envelope. "Who would write to me from Montovia?" She read the first line, then dropped the two-page letter to her lap. "You gotta be kidding!"

"What is it?" Maya leaned forward with interest.

"You were probably right, Maya. It *must* be a scam." Even so, Adelaide picked up the letter. "Although it's surprisingly well done for a scam." She fingered the embossed paper as she held it out for Maya to see. "Official letterhead, good parchment, and it looks like it was typed on a real typewriter."

"Read it out loud," Maya insisted. "If it's a scam, we'll have a good laugh."

Adelaide slowly read from the first page.

Dear Miss Adelaide Katelyn Smith,

With the help of an American investigator, it has come to our attention that you are in all likelihood the direct de-scendant of Maximillian Konig V, reigning king of Mon-tovia. The agency we employed discovered your identity through an international DNA registry. After consulting with several genetic experts, it has been determined that this match is indeed authentic.

We have also confirmed that your late mother, Susan Marie Smith, was engaged to Maximillian Konig V nearly thirty years ago, but the marriage was not approved by the king. According to the investigative report, the engagement was broken, and Ms. Smith returned to the United States. Approximately eight months later, she gave birth to a baby girl named Adelaide Katelyn Smith.

I am writing to inform you that we believe you to be the daughter of King Maximillian Konig V and, as a result, the true royal heir to the throne and—

"Stop, stop, stop!" Maya yelled. "Read that last line again!"

With slightly trembling hands, Adelaide reread that startling sentence. "This *has* to be a scam." She held the letter at arm's length. "Whoever wrote this is seriously twisted." She skimmed the second page of the letter, which detailed an extravagant invitation to Montovia, before she tossed both pages to the floor.

"No way is this real," she declared as she stood. She paced across the small room and mostly ignored Maya, who'd scooped up the letter and was poring over the pages like they were the original draft of the Magna Carta. "This is either an elaborate scam that'll be followed up with a demand for money or someone is playing a prank on me, because there's no possible way this is for real. It's just too weird."

Maya set the pages on the table. "I don't know . . . it seems kind of real to me."

"No way. Things like this don't happen in real life. Seriously, this feels like the plot of a Hallmark movie."

Maya laughed. "Well then, it's a pretty good fake. Maybe someone really is punking you."

Adelaide suddenly remembered the teen girls' weird coffee orders at the end of her shift. Those had been pretty bizarre. Even more over the top than usual . . . and yet Vicki had been quite amused. A light bulb flicked on in her head. Aha! These strange incidents had to be the work of her bosses. Of course! Vicki and Lance were notorious practical jokers. April Fools' Day was their favorite holiday. Yes, they had definitely gotten her with this well-planned charade. Upset over her quitting right before the holidays, they probably wanted to get even and have a good laugh at the same time. Yes, that was the only logical explanation.

Two

Adelaide was still pacing and muttering to herself about Vicki and Lance's poor taste in jokes when Maya interrupted her thoughts.

"Why would they make something like this up?" Maya pointed to the letter on the coffee table. "I mean Montovia is so random. Not to mention extreme." She picked up the envelope and examined the front. "This stamp and postmark look authentic. Like it really came from overseas. Vicki and Lance wouldn't go to this much trouble for a silly practical joke. Seriously? What's the payoff? What's the point?"

"It has to be a scam then. Someone is phishing for money."

Maya snatched up the letter again. "But whoever wrote this hasn't asked for a penny. They only want you to respond and accept their invitation to visit their country. Completely at their expense!"

"Why?"

Maya pointed to the second page of the letter. "It says here that the king is ill, which is why it's imperative you go visit."

"Yes, that's how those scams work. They play on sympathy and make it seem dire. When you agree, they ask you to use your own funds, which they assure you they'll reimburse. But in the meantime, they empty your bank account." She sighed. "Not like there's much in mine to begin with."

Maya held up the letter and read it out loud again. Adelaide hated to admit it but hearing the words read by someone else did make it seem less like a scam or practical joke. But still.

"It's just too weird." Adelaide went to her bookshelf and removed an old atlas. She looked up Montovia and pointed it out to Maya. "See, it's this tiny little country. Right there. Big as a flyspeck."

"Did your mom ever mention it?"

"No. But I do recall hearing about a trip to Europe she and Lela took in college."

"And she never told you anything about your father either, right?"

Adelaide shook her head. "Not a word about my father or Montovia."

"Maybe she wanted it buried." Maya held up a finger. "Hey, why not ask Lela?"

Adelaide considered this. Lela was her mom's best friend in nursing school and had been like an aunt to Adelaide when she was younger. But when she married a naval officer and moved to Maryland to continue her nursing career, she grew a little distant from her old friend. The last time Adelaide had seen Lela was at her mother's funeral three years ago.

"I guess I could call her."

"Yes," Maya urged. "Right now."

Adelaide pulled up Lela's number and, with a slightly shaky finger, clicked call. After a quick exchange of stilted greetings, Adelaide plunged ahead. "Lela, do you remember going to Europe with my mom, back in college?"

After a long pause, Lela answered. "Yes. Of course."

"Was my mom ever in the Principality of Montovia?"

"Why are you asking me this?" Lela sounded uneasy and a bit suspicious, so Adelaide explained the strange letter.

Lela let out a little gasp. "Max was a king?"

"So you *do* know about Max?" Adelaide exchanged glances with Maya.

"Oh, honey, I knew about Max, but that was so long ago I'd almost forgotten him. And yes, your mom and I did spend a month in Europe. It was August. Right before our third year of nursing school. I'd received a small inheritance from my aunt and had always dreamed of touring Europe, so I talked your mom into going as my traveling companion."

"I'm surprised she could afford to go." Adelaide knew how her mom had struggled to make it through school.

"Thanks to my aunt, I was able to cover our expenses, but it was a pretty frugal trip. We were young and carefree. It was fun. And you know how pretty your mom was—kinda like you, Addie. In a blue-eyed and blond way. She was a real head-turner back then. She even got mistaken for Sharon Stone and—"

"Yeah, okay," Adelaide interrupted, "but this Maximillian guy? How did you meet him?"

"We met him in Zurich. Your mom caught his eye, and he invited us out. He spoke great English and insisted on taking us to dinner in this swanky restaurant. The best meal we had in Europe. Heck, it was the best meal we'd had anywhere. Max was obviously very wealthy.

"Our trip was almost over, but your mom still wanted to see Vienna. I said no way. We were short on funds at that point, and our train passes were almost expired. But Max offered to drive us to his family's villa just outside Vienna. I thought it was a bad idea, but your mom insisted we go. I won't deny it was pretty fun. Like *Lifestyles of the Rich and Famous*. But when it was time to go, your mom dragged her heels. Max asked her to stay, and she and I had this huge fight. I was furious, so I just left her there in Vienna."

"Oh." Adelaide's head was spinning. "What happened after that?"

"I honestly don't know what happened with your mom. I was so angry. I got home in time for fall classes and pretty much wrote her off. Later I heard that she came home, but she didn't return to school and we weren't exactly on speaking terms."

"But you patched it up?"

"When I found out she was pregnant, I realized she needed a friend more than ever, so I stepped in. Your mom moved in with my mom until the baby came, but she refused to speak about the circumstances. And we never pushed her. I was there at your birth. After that, my mom babysat you while your mom finished her LPN degree. Not the RPN like she'd originally planned, but at least she could support you two after that."

"Yeah." Adelaide knew how much they'd scrimped to get by. Clipping coupons, riding the transit, shopping at thrift stores.

"I was always surprised she never married."

"She had plenty of opportunities." Adelaide cringed at the memory of some of the guys who'd pursued her mom. As an angst-ridden teenager, Adelaide had even accused her mother of being a "jerk magnet" more than once.

"I guess that's about all I know, Addie."

"But you haven't told me everything." Adelaide took in a steadying breath. "Did you think Max was my father?"

"I'll admit I had my suspicions. But your mom refused to talk about it. *Ever.*"

"Right. Same here. She always got mad if I brought up the paternity subject. She told me not to ask. I used to imagine my dad as a lowlife . . . like a meth addict or a drug dealer or maybe someone who was doing time as a serial killer."

"Oh, that's too bad. I never knew that, honey. I'm so sorry."

"Thanks, Lela." Adelaide took a deep breath, then asked the question that had been rumbling around in her head. "So, this letter—you think it's authentic?"

"Sounds like it, Addie. But for clarity, you are saying that Max is a king?"

"That's what this letter says. He's the king of the Principality of Montovia." Adelaide stared at the page in her hand. "I was almost certain it was a scam at first."

"I never dreamt Max was royalty, but he definitely came from money. He never mentioned royalty or Montovia. Where is that, anyway?"

"It's a tiny country wedged between Austria and Hungary. And you said his family had property in Vienna." She peered down at the still-open atlas. "That's pretty close to Montovia."

"So it sort of makes sense. But do your own research just to be sure."

"Yeah, I'll do an online search."

"May I ask who wrote the letter?"

Adelaide examined the signature. "It's signed by Albert J. Kovacs, prime minister to the Principality of Montovia."

"Certainly sounds official."

"Yeah. There's even an email address to reply to." Adelaide sunk into her chair. "To be honest, I'm sort of in shock. It's a lot to take in."

Maya, still hovering and listening, placed a comforting hand on Adelaide's shoulder.

"I can imagine." Lela released a loud sigh. "So, what are you going to do about it?"

Adelaide nearly dropped her phone. "Do?"

"I mean, if it all pans out and is legit, will you go to Montovia? For a visit? To meet your father?"

"My father? The king?" For some reason the irony made Adelaide giggle. How was it possible she lived in a house that smelled like a dirty litter box, was barely able to cover her rent and buy food beyond ramen noodles . . . and yet she was possibly the daughter of a king? Like a modern-day Cinderella without the stepsisters. Her giggling grew louder until she couldn't help but throw back her head and laugh uncontrollably. She was laughing so hard and hysterically that she had to give Lela a broken goodbye as she rushed across the hall to the bathroom to avoid an embarrassing accident. Cinderella—yeah, right!

Standing in front of the sink of the grimy little bathroom with peeling wallpaper and crumbling linoleum, her giggles turned into tears. She wasn't even sure why. Was she crying for her poor deceased mother? Or her ailing royal father? Or for her confused and somewhat overwhelmed self? Maybe it was for all three. *Oh, Lord*, she prayed silently, *please, help me figure this puzzle out.*

Three

B y the next day, Adelaide had done enough research to know that her letter from Montovia was most likely legitimate. King Maximillian V was listed as the ruler of the principality, and Albert J. Kovacs was the prime minister serving under him. Informative emails between Kovacs and Adelaide passed back and forth across the ocean until, a few days later, she received a registered letter containing her temporary visa to Montovia, as well as a cashier's check to cover all travel expenses.

"You *have* to go," Maya told her as they both stared at the generous check. "It's meant to be."

"Meant to be?" Adelaide tossed her winter coat onto a peg by the door.

"Well, you said you prayed about it, right?"

"Yeah . . ." Adelaide sank down into her favorite well-worn chair.

"Well, it looks like God has flung the door wide open."

Adelaide considered this. "What about school? My finals?"

"It wouldn't be the first time you've delayed your education. And look what an opportunity you're being given to travel."

Maya sat across from her. "Not to mention the chance to meet your birth father who just happens to rule a small country. Seriously, isn't that like an education in itself?"

Adelaide set the check on the crate coffee table. "You're probably right."

"And I'll bet your passport is still good. Weren't you twenty when you and your mom took that trip to Canada?"

She nodded. "Yeah. Almost nine years ago. I have a little over a year before it expires."

"See, it's meant to be."

Adelaide couldn't argue. Oh, she could've, but why waste her breath? Besides that, Maya was right. Traveling and visiting a place like Montovia *was* a form of education. She picked up the check again and stared at the numbers. "This looks like more than enough to cover airfare."

"And travel expenses," Maya added.

"Okay."

Adelaide's flight was booked exactly one week after receiving her first mysterious Montovian letter . . . and just a few days after she received a disturbing email informing her that King Maximillian V was possibly on his deathbed. There was no time to waste. By now she knew he suffered a prolonged case of liver cancer, but Herr Kovacs had encouraged him to hold out long enough to lay eyes on his daughter. Herr Kovacs seemed to think it was helping, but the doctor's prognosis was grim.

As Adelaide flew across the ocean in the darkness of night, she fervently prayed she'd get the opportunity to meet her father in person before it was too late. Based on Herr Kovacs's email earlier in the day, the king was going downhill quickly. Time was of the essence.

Her plane arrived at Vienna International Airport just as

dawn gently broke into the sullen gray sky. As Adelaide hovered near the passenger pick-up area, she checked her phone for a new message from Herr Kovacs and then noticed today's date. Tomorrow would be the third anniversary of her mother's passing. It was a night Adelaide didn't care to remember and always brought memory of a painful phone call she had tried to wipe clean from her mind. Weary from the red-eye flight and staring down at that familiar date, she couldn't stop it from all rushing back.

Her mother had gone out with one of those jerks who always seemed to pursue her so relentlessly. Sure, according to her mom, Terrance was different. He had a respectable job, a nice dog, and was easy on the eyes—but his alcohol level had been .40 when autopsies were performed on him and Adelaide's mother in the days to follow. No other cars had been involved in the accident, and both the driver and passenger had died instantly when the sporty BMW left the road and crashed into a tree.

"Frau Smith?"

Adelaide looked up from her daze and blinked. The dark-haired young man addressing her didn't match the picture she had in her head of the prime minister she'd been corresponding with, but he held a placard with her name printed on it. "Herr Kovacs? Sind sie das?" She nervously straightened the front of her long gray coat, hoping her high school German wasn't too awful.

"Nein. Ich bin Anton Balazs. Herr Kovacs schickte mir." His broad smile was encouraging, but he spoke too quickly. Other than "nein" for "no," she couldn't make out a word. She fumbled to discreetly locate her phone's translation app, then realized it was useless.

"Mein Deutsch ist not gut." She spoke slowly, embarrassed to confess her poor language skills.

"My apologies. Please, let's converse in English," he said, lowering the sign. "I'll start again. I'm Anton Balazs. Herr Kovacs has sent me to meet you." He extended his hand, then warmly grasped hers.

"I'm pleased to meet you, Herr Balazs. You speak English fluently?"

"Yes. German is our national language, but Montovian children start to learn English in primary school. It's because Queen Anna Konig was British. That was nearly a century ago, but her insistence that English be required in the curriculum remained, even ahead of French and Hungarian."

"Well, I commend you, Herr Balazs. Your English is excellent."

"It helped that my mother was British, plus I attended Cambridge." His dark brown eyes twinkled. "But please, dispose of *herr*. Just call me Anton."

"Then you must call me Adelaide."

"And I hope you forgive Albert—I mean, Herr Kovacs for not coming this morning. I call him Albert because he is my uncle. He was very concerned for the king's health and insisted on remaining behind."

"Yes, I've heard the king is unwell. I'm sorry."

"My uncle is with him now."

"Then we should probably hurry." She reached for her roller suitcase handle.

"Let me get that. Have you checked luggage?"

"No." She let him take the case while looping the strap of her oversized bag over one shoulder.

"You travel light."

She shrugged. "This trip was such short notice, I didn't have time to think about it." Or more truthfully, her closet had always been sparse. And, although she'd bought a few new things to bring along, she would never be mistaken for a clotheshorse.

"The car is that way." Anton nodded toward the exit. "It's a three-hour drive to Horvath, but we decided a car would be faster than waiting for a train."

"Horvath? The capital of Montovia?"

"Yes. The palace has been there for ages, probably since the fourteenth century. It was most likely Hungarian then, although historians never seem to agree." He continued educating her about his home country as they walked. "Horvath has been home to the Montovian royal family for more than three hundred years." He paused at the sliding doors for her to exit ahead of him, waiting like a gentleman.

"And Montovia is comprised of three provinces, not including the capital?" she asked as they stood on the sidewalk.

"You've been reading up on us." He waved toward the row of waiting cars.

"I like knowledge." She felt her eyes grow wide as a black limousine pulled up and a uniformed man hopped out to take her bags. Anton opened her door, then waited as she got in. She felt like pinching herself as she slid onto the luxurious leather seat. So Hollywood! As Anton got in on the other side, she glanced through the tinted windows, wondering whether anyone was watching. Sure enough, a few bystanders pointed in their direction with curious expressions.

"Are you hungry?" Anton asked as the limo pulled back into the airport traffic.

"Hungry?" She was starving but didn't want to delay their travels with a stop for food. "I thought we were in a hurry."

"You're right. But my mother had something prepared for us, just in case." He slid a handsome picnic basket between them, then opened it to display pretty porcelain dishes, cloth napkins, and gleaming silverware fastened to the lid. A few food items were neatly tucked below, but Anton reached in and removed a silver thermos. "Coffee?"

"I'd love some."

Before long they were dining on delicious pastries, hard-boiled eggs, fresh fruit, and creamy cheese. It couldn't have been a more welcome feast. "I feel like a princess," she said as he refilled her coffee cup and added cream.

He chuckled. "You *are* a princess."

Her face grew warm. "Oh, but not really. I mean, I realize it appears the king is my father based on some DNA tests, but my mother was never married to him. I hardly think anyone would regard *me* as a princess."

"That's where you might be wrong." He opened a small foil-covered box. "Bonbon?"

"Seriously?" Each delicate chocolate had a different Christmas symbol on top—tiny candy canes, holly swags, bells. "These are so Christmassy. They're too pretty to eat."

"You don't want to try one?" He waved the box temptingly.

"I'd love to." She took an evergreen tree bonbon and bit into it. "Delicious!"

"These are my mother's favorites. From a chocolatier in Horvath."

"I'll have to pay that shop a visit while I'm here."

"Yes, you should enjoy seeing the whole village." Anton set the bonbon box on the seat between them. "Shops are just starting to prepare for Christmas. By the weekend, the whole village will be lit up and sparkling. All of Montovia celebrates the season with great enthusiasm, but Horvath puts on the best show. It goes throughout December and ends on New Year's."

She sighed. "I can hardly believe it's almost December." She tried not to think of the exams she'd rescheduled for January as she peered out the window at the countryside. They'd been driving through gorgeous rolling hills and past blue mountain lakes, but now it seemed they were headed into more rugged terrain. "It's so beautiful here. Are those mountains the Alps?"

Anton leaned toward Adelaide to look through her window. "That is a matter of opinion. Our mountains connect to the Alps, but some mountain snobs refuse to call them the Alps. Montovians will tell you that our country is actually nestled in the foot of the Alps at an elevation just over 1,200 meters."

"Does that mean snow for Christmas?" she asked eagerly.

"You can usually count on it." Anton leaned back in the seat, gazing her way with a sideways glance. "You resemble your father, Adelaide."

"Really?" She turned to face him. "Some think I look like my mother. Although she was fairer."

"Your green eyes are strikingly similar to your father's, and the king's hair used to be a rich warm brown like yours, but it's grown quite gray these past few years." His expression grew somber. "He has aged beyond his years."

"Because of the illness?"

He frowned. "That is one theory."

"Meaning there is another?"

"Perhaps." His tone sounded a bit crisp, as if he regretted his words.

Cradling the white porcelain coffee cup in her hand, she let the warmth seep into her fingers before she decided to press her host a bit more. "I've read everything I could find about Montovia in the last few days. Sort of like doing my homework." She smiled. "But there's not a lot of information online. I'd love to hear more. Especially about my, uh, the king." She couldn't bring herself to call Maximillian V her father. Of course, she would have difficulty calling anyone "Father," not to mention a complete stranger.

"Right." Anton nodded sagely. "I should probably fill you in on the recent family history. The king was a bachelor for quite some time. Of course, it was expected he would marry. According to my uncle, his parents urged him to wed many a time, but King Maximillian was stubborn. Uncle Albert believes it's because of his love for your mother, that he never got over her. My uncle got to meet your mother when she visited our country all those years ago. Albert says she was a beauty, but not only that. He believes she was a genuinely good and kind person."

"I agree with him. As a nurse my mother was always very

29

kind to all her patients . . . to everyone, really." Perhaps too kind to some people . . . like Terrance. But she didn't care to mention that.

"Your mother was a nurse?"

"Yes. Until she died."

"I've been doing my homework too. I read of your mother's tragic accident. I'm so sorry for your loss."

"It'll be three years tomorrow."

"Tomorrow? Really?"

She sighed.

For a moment, Anton was quiet.

"I can't explain it," Adelaide said, "but somehow I think Mom would approve of me coming here. She never spoke of my, uh, my father. I think the story was buried deep within her. In fact, she never married."

"I'm aware of that." He frowned. "I also know the king tried to find her for years. For the record, he never knew she was with child. And with the somewhat common name of Susan Smith, and not knowing where she lived in the States, well, it proved a challenge. If you hadn't been listed on that DNA network, we never would've known about you. Did you join the registry in hopes of discovering your father?"

"I did it last summer in a moment of weakness. I was lonely for some sort of family connection. My mother had no interest in the registry. I suspect she wanted to protect our anonymity. She was a proud woman, and I think being rejected by Max, or his family, well, I'm sure it broke her heart." This was something that Adelaide was still processing, but it made sense, like missing puzzle pieces slipping into place.

"And yet she named you Adelaide Katelyn."

She cocked her head to the side. "Why do you say that?"

"Didn't you know King Maximillian's mother was Adelaide Katelin?"

"Really?" She blinked a few times. "I had no idea."

"Your middle names are spelt a bit differently. Yours has a *Y* where hers has an *I*."

"Interesting." Although she felt tired from lack of sleep, this conversation kept nudging her wakefulness.

"According to my uncle, the former queen liked your mother. She approved the marriage. It was her husband, Maximillian IV, who forbade the union of your parents."

"I see." Adelaide felt indignation for her mother. Such rejection would hurt.

"It was also Maximillian IV who pressured his son to eventually marry a different woman about eighteen years ago."

"Is that Queen Johanna? I don't recall her full name."

"Queen Johanna Maria Egger Bohm Konig. She was widowed by Prime Minister Georg Bohm about twenty years ago. King Maximillian, with no heir, decided Johanna and her fifteen-year-old son were a good fit for a ready-made royal family. She was an attractive and well-respected woman, but not one particularly known for her warmth."

"I see."

"Queen Johanna never bore royal offspring and consequently nurtures aspirations for her own son to inherit the throne."

Adelaide didn't know how to respond to that, so she decided to change the subject. "Tell me more about the king. Has he been a good ruler?"

"Very good. He's only been on the throne for sixteen years, but the country has flourished under the wise reign of King Max."

"Is that what he goes by? King Max?"

"Yes, he encouraged the name shortly after he was crowned, and the people love it. He's a natural leader."

"But that has changed now that he's grown ill?"

Anton shook his head. "Even in his illness, his country always comes first."

"And what about Queen Johanna? I know you mentioned

31

her son, but why wouldn't she take over leadership when King Max is gone?"

"I'm sure she would like that, and we've had queens on the throne before, but according to law, the ruler should be a direct descendant of the royal family."

"I see."

"The king has a brother, more than ten years his junior, who would have been next in line."

"*Would* have?"

"Yes. Prince Farcus has been missing for about six weeks." Sadness reflected in his eyes. "King Max is very distraught over it."

"What happened to him?"

"Prince Farcus went to Scotland on a fishing trip and never came back."

"Do you think it was an accident?"

His expression suggested uncertainty. "The rumor that he drowned has circulated."

"But you don't think so?"

Anton shrugged. "I have my doubts."

"Does Prince Farcus have a wife? Perhaps a domestic situation he wished to escape?"

"No. He is unmarried and childless."

Adelaide considered this. "Perhaps his disappearance is his way of saying he doesn't wish for the responsibility of the throne. He has no interest in ruling Montovia?"

"Some believe that, but I know your uncle fairly well. He is a free spirit and sometimes questions the practicality of monarchy in the modern age. But cowardice does not fit his character. He is a good man. We've sent inquiries and investigators to Scotland to search for him, but with no results, no leads, nothing."

"How mysterious."

"Very. Naturally, with Prince Farcus missing and King Max's health failing, Queen Johanna feels more certain than ever that her son, who's been legally adopted by the king, should be next in line for the crown."

"Despite what you said about bloodlines?"

"Yes, it's possible that Parliament could vote to make an exception due to Georg's legal adoption."

"How old is Georg?" Adelaide asked.

"He's a few years younger than I am. But he seems younger to me."

She studied his expression. "Do you question his ability to rule?"

"I do not care to say." Anton was hard to read, but Adelaide suspected he was holding something back. Perhaps for diplomacy's sake. Regardless, the message was clear—Anton felt Prince Georg wouldn't make a good ruler.

"May I ask your opinion of the queen? You insinuated she was a bit cool." Adelaide knew she was fishing but felt she could trust this man. "What should I expect when I meet her?"

He rubbed his chin. "She is an extremely strong woman. Intelligent and well-spoken. She presents a very regal image and is popular with some." Although his words mostly praised the queen, his eyes betrayed him.

Adelaide noted his apparent distaste for the queen, then asked another question. "And you say that she's very eager for Georg to inherit the throne?"

Eyes downward, he nodded.

"So, I expect Queen Johanna will not welcome me with open arms."

Anton looked amused. "To be honest, Queen Johanna doesn't even know about you . . . or your impending visit."

"What?" Adelaide sat up straight. "Won't that be awkward?"

"My uncle thought it best. I don't want to suggest the queen is malevolent, but between you and me, she is a bit self-serving and"—he cleared his throat—"we believe she is capable of intricate schemes to her own benefit."

"Really?"

"I hadn't planned to disclose this much, but it seems only fair to give you warning." He leaned forward. "Be on your guard with the queen."

Adelaide tilted her head to one side. "Are you suggesting she's dangerous?"

"Not in a physical sense, but she's been known to make life difficult for people who oppose her."

Adelaide felt somewhat challenged by the thought of having a good argument with Queen Johanna. "That could be amusing."

He smiled. "I'm glad you think so. I have a feeling you'll be a worthy opponent to the queen. I know you're studying law. That could prove a valuable asset."

"Maybe." Adelaide couldn't help but suppress a sleepy yawn. Despite her interest in this conversation, the combination of good food and a warm car ride was making her drowsy.

It did not escape Anton's notice. "I didn't mean to talk your ear off. I'm sure you're worn-out from your flight." Anton lifted the seat between them and pulled out a woolly plaid blanket. "Feel free to have some rest," he said, handing it to her. "You'll need your strength and wits about you when we arrive."

"Thank you." She snuggled down with the blanket and began to consider all the people and circumstances he'd just described to her as puzzle pieces. How would they fit, or not fit, into a fuller picture? But not having slept for more than twenty-four hours, her mind was not clear or clever at the moment. And so she leaned back and closed her eyes and silently asked the Lord to lead her through what came next.

CHAPTER

Four

It took Adelaide a moment to get her bearings when she opened her eyes a while later. Anton was still sitting beside her, his focus on his laptop. He didn't notice she was awake, so she took a moment to study him carefully. He mentioned that she was a few years younger than he was, so what would that make him? Maybe midthirties? Possibly, but he seemed to possess something that she'd been accused of having more than a few times—an old soul. His face had a boyish quality, though the dark-framed glasses he'd donned while she napped made him seem older—or maybe just more studious? All in all, he was a very attractive man.

Despite all the information he'd dispensed upon her, she really knew very little about him personally. His mother was British, he'd gone to Cambridge, and his uncle was a prime minister. She knew he worked with his uncle but was unsure of his job title . . . or if he was married. Of course, his personal life was irrelevant and none of her business, but just the same, she was curious.

"You're awake." He smiled, removing his glasses and rubbing the bridge of his nose. "And just in time." He nodded toward the window on his side. "You'll be getting your first peek at the palace after we go around this next curve."

"Really?" She peered out to see a rugged hillside draped in low-hanging banks of fog. Very mysterious.

"We've been in Montovia for a couple of hours," he said. "I almost woke you when we passed through my province, but you were sleeping so soundly."

"Your province?"

"Yes. Gruber. It's very mountainous and beautiful, but it is the poorest province of Montovia. Although it has, I believe, the richest people. Not monetarily, but in spirit and determination and kindness. Our little village, Marie Folyam, is quite charming. Very small and old-fashioned."

She sat up and stretched. "Oh, I wish I'd seen it."

"Perhaps you will someday." He pointed out his window. "There, can you see the palace through the fog? Up on that hill there?"

She leaned toward him to look out. "Oh my goodness, it looks absolutely magical! Like a fairy-tale castle!" She studied the high stone walls and turrets, all topped with russet tiles. "It's so beautiful. I almost don't have words for it."

"I think I mentioned it was first built in the fourteenth century, but it's been added to and renovated several times. Most recently in the 1960s to modernize plumbing and electric."

"Well, it looks amazing. Like something from an old Disney movie."

He chuckled. "Queen Johanna has suggested renting it for movie productions, but King Max is opposed to that idea. The queen is also keen to develop tourism in Montovia, but again, the king is not so inclined."

"I'm glad. It looks like such a special place. It'd be a shame to commercialize it." As the limo rounded another corner, the fairy-tale scene disappeared from view. "Is the queen concerned about Montovia's finances? Is that why she wants to create revenue?"

Anton seemed to consider this before responding. "I'm sure that's part of it, although Montovia is fiscally stable. But I also know the queen enjoys social events, public relations, and just generally being in the spotlight."

"Seems fitting for a queen."

He nodded with a slightly grim expression. Adelaide knew he was trying to maintain diplomacy while still tipping her off. She appreciated it. As they continued through the rolling green countryside, she admired what appeared to be numerous vineyards, interspersed with small farms and pastures of sheep and cows and haystacks. Some of the homes had thatched roofs. All were charmingly bucolic and picturesque. But soon farm properties were replaced with estates, large houses, and landscaped yards.

"These homes look more modern than the farmhouses we just passed," Adelaide said.

"And more costly too."

"I noticed. You mentioned your province wasn't too well-off. Is Hovarth much wealthier?"

"The Hovarth province is considered a more desirable place to live. In 1985, King Maximillian IV followed Liechtenstein's lead by eliminating income tax. The government is sustained through property tax. As a result, we now have a continual influx of very wealthy landowners. Some who live here year-round and some who come seasonally. Hovarth enjoys more of this revenue than the other two provinces."

She wanted to ask if he thought this fair and equitable, but he was pointing to a sign up ahead. "Now we're coming into Horvath proper."

She read the sign aloud: "Welcome to Hovarth. Capital of the Principality of Montovia. Established 1698. Population 1,854." She turned toward him, her eyes wide. "Goodness, that's not very big."

"Believe it or not, it's the largest village in Montovia. The whole province of Hovarth, including this village, holds a third of the country's entire population."

"Yes, I remember reading that Montovia's population is less than fifteen thousand. Not even as big as the university I attended." Adelaide tried to wrap her head around a country this small. Charming but strange.

The road wound past more fancy homes with large, beautiful yards and high ornate gates. Soon they were passing much smaller and older chalet-like homes on town-size lots. The houses grew taller, but nothing was over four stories. These buildings were all connected, suggesting they were within the central part of town. Suddenly they were traveling down a narrow cobblestone street, right through a picturesque village.

"Look, you can see some of the shopkeepers are already getting ready for Christmas." Anton waved to a man on a ladder hanging a string of lights. "The village Christmas tree will go up over there." He pointed to the village square. "That happens the first day of December. This Friday night, there'll be a big party right here. After the tree lights are turned on, there'll be food, music, carol singing, dancing."

"How fun!"

"It's always been the king's responsibility to turn on the lights, but it's doubtful he'll be well enough this year."

She frowned. "Who will do it?"

"I heard Queen Johanna and Prince Georg plan to handle it."

She nodded solemnly. That was the first time she'd heard Anton refer to the queen's son as *Prince* Georg, but it was probably his proper title. She continued to stare out her window as they passed quaint shops and businesses. She tried to fight back the suspicion that she'd just traveled through a time warp and was transported a few centuries back in time. Of course, the people's modern clothing and small cars didn't fit this illusion, but all in all, it was a curious blast from the past. She briefly considered pulling out her phone to take photos, but she'd never been the type to obsess over pictures. She poked fun at those who posed at every interval, photographing food from all angles until it got cold.

As the limo ascended the road to the palace, Adelaide could see it looked even prettier close up. The stone walls, a warm wheat tone, were set off by the russet-red tiles on the varied rooflines above. Though the palace had a stalwart appearance, it was also welcoming. As they got closer, an ornate iron gate opened automatically to let them into a large, protected court-yard area. A few other vehicles were parked about, but Adelaide could just imagine horses and carts from a bygone era.

Of course, as Anton used his cell phone to speak to some-one inside, she was reminded of the current century. The limo driver dropped them off in front of an intricately carved wooden door, flanked by enormous arched windows with stained glass. Standing outside the door was a colorfully uniformed porter. He greeted them and opened the massive door with flourish and ease. Although it was chilly here, Adelaide knew her goose bumps had nothing to do with the temperature. Was this place for real? Was she actually here . . . or just dreaming?

"This is the ground floor," Anton told her as they entered into a large entry hall. A few tapestries and oversize paintings of historic aristocracy lined the stone walls, as well as some old furnishings. In the center was a massive staircase that fanned invitingly out onto the marble floor. "This level is mostly utili-tarian. It includes servants' quarters, storage, laundry, access to the stables and gardens and such. This hall has probably seen the least change over the recent centuries." He pointed to a set of carved wooden doors. "However, there is an elevator."

"An elevator? That staircase is so beautiful, why would you want to use an elevator?"

He laughed. "You wouldn't if you're young and strong and energetic. Would you like to take the stairs?"

"Most definitely."

As they climbed the stairs, which were more numerous than a usual staircase, Anton explained what lay on the next floor. "We call it the first floor, and it's something of a public space. Primarily used for business or entertaining. A large ballroom is off to the left, and the formal dining room, which seats more than thirty guests, is opposite. There's also a spacious sitting room, a well-stocked library, a meeting room, and several parliamentary and prime ministerial offices. I'd offer you the full tour, but I feel compelled to get you to King Max promptly. He's on the third floor."

Adelaide paused in the center of the first floor's elegant entry hall. Warmed by the climb, she removed her long coat and draped it over her arm as she took in her surroundings. This floor was much better lit than the one below. The huge crystal chandelier, combined with more stained glass windows, flooded the marble-floored hall with color and light.

"Very nice," she murmured, turning to Anton. She could feel him studying her, perhaps critiquing her very lawyer-like ensemble, which suddenly felt out of place in this sophisticated place. The white button-down shirt, gray cashmere cardigan, straight black wool skirt, and black ankle boots had felt practically stylish yesterday. Not so much now. She forced a smile. "Should we take the elevator to expedite things?"

"Yes." He went over to push the button. "I already notified the king's aide that we were on our way up." As they got in, he described the floor that they were skipping. "Eight very comfortable guest rooms occupy one side. Six that are en suite, two that share a bath. There's also a sitting room for guest use. The other side is primarily used for smaller gatherings. A large parlor, a semiformal dining room, and another library."

"Is the third floor the top floor?"

"As far as living quarters go, yes. But there are several interesting spots in the turrets above. They are only accessible by steep stairs and rather like crow's nests, but the views are spectacular." He checked his watch. "The third floor is for royal family use only. The king's suite is the largest room and has its own private study. The queen's suite is much smaller, but she utilizes an attached nursery. There are also two bedrooms for family members, an intimate but comfortable sitting room, and a smaller dining room and separate kitchen."

"Interesting. It sounds like a complete house all on one floor."

"Yes, very self-contained and comfortable. Best of all, in my opinion, are the terraces and views. Especially from the king's quarters."

As the elevator doors opened, Adelaide was assaulted by a surge of nerves. "Am I supposed to act a certain way?" she whispered. "Do I bow or curtsy or—"

"Don't worry. Montovia is not as formal as Great Britain. And don't forget, you are royalty too."

She shook her head in disbelief. *Royalty?* How was that possible? But there was no time for more questions, because a dignified middle-aged man in a dark gray suit was approaching them. He greeted Anton, then waited to be introduced to Adelaide. Anton introduced the man as Herr Schneider, the king's assistant. She did not miss that Herr Schneider politely dipped his head—like a bow.

"King Max is waiting." The king's assistant turned, then led them down a slightly dim hallway until he came to a tall wooden door, where he tapped three times and, using a key, opened it.

Herr Schneider stood aside as Adelaide stepped toward the door. As if noticing her nervousness, Anton spoke softly behind her. "I'll wait in the library. Let me take that for you." He removed her coat from her arm. "Don't worry, you'll be fine."

She looked at him with wide eyes, not willing to part ways with her congenial guide. "But I—"

He placed a comforting hand on her arm. "King Max wishes a private conversation with you."

"Does he speak English?" she asked, her heart beating quickly.

"Fluently." His bright smile felt like a small shot of courage.

Adelaide took a deep breath as she followed Herr Schneider into a fairly normal-looking sitting room. But she noticed the many details that made it more than an everyday space. Thick pale blue carpeting, walls painted an even paler shade of blue, beautiful oil landscapes with ornate gold-gilded frames. She also spotted several well-arranged pieces of contemporary and antique furnishings complemented by attractive accents, but it was the tall arched back of the royal blue velveteen chair that captured her full attention.

It faced away from her, toward a large window with an amazing view of the countryside. She knew that her father was seated in that chair. *Her father . . . the king.* She felt slightly faint.

CHAPTER

Five

Herr Schneider politely presented Adelaide to King Max, then indicated she should sit in the armchair opposite him. With trembling knees, she eased herself into it, gripping the soft velvet in her nervousness. Neither of them spoke as the king's assistant quietly made his exit, locking the door behind him. Adelaide felt she could barely breathe, let alone speak. Besides, she wondered, perhaps it was impolite to speak first. She ran her hands over her plain wool skirt, crossing her legs at the ankles and tucking them beneath the chair the way Maya had taught her to do back in middle school. Still, the king did not speak. He simply looked at her with a somber expression that was impossible to read. Was he disappointed, regretful, concerned, or just plain weary?

She returned his gaze, using her own poker face, and was surprised to see that Anton was right—his eyes, though paler, were strikingly similar to hers. And although his hair was partly gray, she could see dark brown strands mixed in. Like her hair, it was wavy, a bit on the longish side, but perhaps he'd been too ill to see a barber. He was dressed in navy trousers and a quilted maroon jacket with a gold crest—was that what they called a smoking jacket?—she thought he looked quite regal. But his leather slippers looked worn.

It was his skin tone that bothered her. At first, she'd thought he was simply tanned by the sun, but on closer inspection, she noticed he appeared very jaundiced. Probably from his failing liver. She cleared her throat, thinking it might be polite to inquire of his health. But he spoke first.

"Adelaide Katelin." He spoke her name, with tenderness, in a German accent. "You know, that was my mother's name."

"I just learned that from Anton— I mean, Herr Balazs."

He waved a hand. "Is all right. You call him Anton. He is good boy, no?"

She nodded with a nervous smile.

"You look like your mother." His voice sounded husky. He fumbled for his jacket pocket and extracted a linen handkerchief, which he used to dab the corners of his eyes. "I know she is gone . . . too soon. I am sorry for your loss, mein lieber."

"Thank you." She knew *mein lieber* meant "my dear," and she was touched to be called such a sweet term of endearment. "I loved my mother very much. And I miss her still."

"Ja." He sighed. "I still miss my mutter, and I am old."

She wasn't sure how old he was but suspected he looked older than his years.

"She never married?" His emerald eyes probed into hers. "Is that true?"

"That's true."

"And she never spoke of me?" His head tilted toward her in a way that suggested vulnerability. "You *never* knew of me?"

Adelaide pursed her lips, realizing how much she suddenly wanted to protect him. Didn't want to hurt him. "It was her secret."

He nodded slowly. "Ja. Her secret." He gazed past her now, toward the window, but she sensed he was looking much farther away, beyond the landscape out there. For another long moment neither of them spoke.

"I am glad you came, Adelaide." He smiled and, like the sun breaking through the clouds, his face lit up as he held his hands up at arm's length. "I welcome you to Montovia. What do you think of our small principality?"

"It's beautiful! The mountains, the rolling hills, the little farms with meadows full of sheep and cows—it's all so picturesque. And the village looks perfectly charming. I can't wait to explore the shops. And this palace is like . . ." She trailed off, searching for more sophisticated words. "It's like a fairy tale."

He clapped his hands happily. "That is exactly what your mother say when she come here." His smile faded. "If only she stayed."

Adelaide didn't know what to say. How could her mother have possibly remained in a country where the king had wanted her out?

"I begged her to stay."

She felt confused. "But your father . . . I thought he disapproved."

"He did disapprove. But I told Susan we would marry anyway."

"What about your—"

"I have a brother. Prince Farcus could rule. He was only a boy then, but by the time our father passed, Farcus was a man. He could've taken the crown in my stead."

"You would have given up the crown for my mother?"

He nodded solemnly. "I loved her."

"Did my mother know this?"

"I told her." He held his palms upward. "Susan said I would come to regret it. She left without a word. Nothing. My mother confessed, much later, that my father helped her to go."

"Do you think he told her to be quiet about her relationship with you? Perhaps even paid her off? Is that why she kept it a secret?"

"It is possible." He leaned back in his chair with a weary sigh.

"Or perhaps she kept quiet out of her love for you." Adelaide preferred to believe this. After all, as far as she knew, her mother had never had money.

He brightened slightly, but his eyes looked sad, or maybe just tired.

"I know you've been ill. I don't want to wear you out with too much—"

"You do not wear me out," he said, cutting her off. "You are fresh air and sunshine. Good food and excellent wine. You make me feel well. I am so very glad you are here."

She smiled. "I'm very glad I'm here too."

"Tell me about yourself, Adelaide. Your life, your interests."

Without painting too pitiful a picture of her somewhat deprived childhood, she gave him a brief biography of her life and accomplishments. "And I'm nearly finished with law school."

"My daughter a lawyer?" Pride shone in his eyes.

"I hope."

"You do not speak of your love life. Such a beautiful young woman . . . is there no man?"

She shrugged. "Oh, I was involved with a guy for a few years, but his plans were different than mine. We went our separate ways." She didn't care to go into details over Brent's insistence that they move in together . . . or that she'd been holding out for an engagement ring. It was all water under the bridge now.

"You spoke of Anton Balazs." His brows arched and his eyes twinkled. "He is a handsome fellow—a very good man. Just a little older than you."

Using her poker face, she simply nodded. "A valuable and helpful friend, no doubt."

"Anton is the youngest member of Parliament."

"He told me he works with his uncle, but he didn't mention Parliament." She couldn't help but feel impressed.

"He is a humble man who represents a humble province."

"He spoke fondly of his province."

"His uncle is a good man too. I trust Albert Kovacs like a brother."

"Speaking of brothers . . ." She instantly regretted her words, because his eyes grew very sad, and he reached for his handkerchief.

"I do not know what has become of Farcus," he told her. "Albert has hired investigators, but no one is able to find him. I fear he is dead."

She leaned forward, peering curiously at him. "But if he died on the fishing trip in Scotland, wouldn't you have been notified?"

He slowly shook his head. "I do not know. Some are certain he has drowned. Maybe in a boating accident."

"With no witnesses, no evidence, no body? That doesn't make sense."

"Prince Georg blames the Loch Ness Monster." He scowled.

"You don't believe that, do you?"

"No." He looked more tired than ever, and Adelaide got out of her chair so she could kneel by his side. She took his hand.

"I'm sorry to have troubled you. Please, don't worry. Perhaps your brother is simply enjoying an extended vacation. Maybe he met someone and plans to bring home a new wife. Wouldn't that be nice?"

King Max smiled, clasping her hand with both of his. "You are good medicine, mein lieber. But you are right in your assessment. I *am* tired. Let me rest. You come back to dine with me . . . at six? I keep da hours of der Greis—a very old man. You come back then, ja?"

"Ja. I will see you at six." She leaned over to kiss his cheek, which probably surprised her more than him, because he simply leaned back, closed his eyes, and smiled.

She stood and quietly slipped out to see both the king's aide and a uniformed nurse waiting with anxious expressions. She was barely out the door before they hurried past her to check on the king. She went back down the dimly lit hallway, hoping that Anton had stuck around like he'd promised. The youngest member of Parliament and he'd never said a word.

"There you are." He came up from behind her in the entry hall. "Your visit was longer than we expected. I was just talking to my uncle." He pocketed his phone. "Did the visit go well?"

"I, uh, I think so." She felt on the verge of tears, wishing that she, like the king, had a clean white handkerchief tucked in her pocket.

"Your things have been placed in your room." He put his elbow out for her to take. "I'll show you where that is and, if you are willing, I'll wait while you take a moment to freshen up and then I will take you to lunch."

She wrapped her arm over his. "Thank you." His kindness stirred even more emotion.

"That is the library." He pointed to a set of double doors. "I'll wait for you there." Now he led her down a different hallway, past a couple of rooms. "This will be your room." He pointed to a door.

"On this floor?" she asked. "I thought this was the royal family's—"

"You are part of the royal family, Princess Adelaide."

She fought to contain her tears, but instead of arguing with him, she opened the door to her room and stepped inside. He probably thought she was rude as she firmly closed the door behind her, but she felt raw . . . as if the top layer of her skin had been peeled away and the slightest touch would cause pain. This was too much . . . too hard . . . too soon.

A delaide had never considered herself an overly emotional person. After all, a successful attorney knows how to hold feelings in, keep them at bay, and play their best poker face. Yet after a good cry, she felt better. And after a refreshing shower in a bathroom that came fully stocked with the best aromatic amenities, she was almost ready to face the world again.

Wrapped in a thick terry robe, she decided to really check out her luxurious suite. She'd never been fond of pink, but the pale shell-pink color of the walls was calming. The walls were artfully decorated with lovely paintings of pastures and sheep and mountains. The large portrait of a shepherdess that hung above the headboard was her favorite. It felt so familiar to her, she wondered if it might've been an ancestor.

As she padded about the spacious bedroom, the dove-gray carpeting was soothing beneath her bare feet. Her clothes had all been neatly unpacked and put away by someone while she met with the king, but they barely made a dent on the generous closet and large bureau of drawers. As she flipped through her options, trying to choose something appropriate for the afternoon, she knew her wardrobe was at best very limited. She finally pulled on her nicest pair of black slacks and an olive turtleneck. Boring perhaps, but at least the garments, which she'd found in her favorite thrift store, were good quality. She added a paisley silk scarf to her ensemble. Although it helped, its somber burgundy tones were not exactly festive. But then, neither was she.

Adelaide ran a hand over the ornately hand-carved bed frame. Like the other wood furnishings, it had darkened with age and was probably centuries old. She carried her boots over to the creamy white armchair. With its matching ottoman, it was clearly not an antique. She sunk into its soft comfort to pull on her boots, longing to linger there. It would provide the perfect place to read a book or gaze out the window. But she couldn't keep Anton waiting.

She went over to the bed to grab her long winter coat. The fluffy duvet and pillows looked inviting, promising a good night's sleep. Like the king, she would be keeping "old folks" hours tonight—and was glad of it. How long had it been since she'd slept in a real bed? She couldn't calculate the hours since she'd gotten on the plane back home. As she reached for her bag, she couldn't deny this room truly was fit for royalty. Although she did not feel the least bit princess-like. But perhaps that didn't matter.

Anton was waiting as promised in the library. She apologized for taking so long, but he quickly dismissed it. "My only responsibility for the day is to see that you are well cared for," he said as he headed for the elevator. "I made a lunch reservation in the village. Do you mind if we go directly there? I can give you a full tour of the palace when we return."

"Lunch sounds lovely."

As they went down, Anton asked if she preferred to go by limousine or his vehicle, and Adelaide admitted that she liked the anonymity of a less conspicuous car. He seemed to appreciate that. Before long, she was climbing into his older Land Rover and was glad she'd worn pants.

"I know we could've eaten in the palace, but you'll probably be there a fair amount of time anyway—if King Max gets his way, that is."

"I'd like to spend as much time with him as possible," she confessed.

"I'm glad to hear that." He asked about her visit, and she explained that they'd barely started to get acquainted, but she felt it had been good.

"Herr Schneider seemed impressed."

"Impressed how?"

"He said the king was in very good spirits after your visit. Schneider and the nurse had to almost force him to take his afternoon rest. But hopes of dining with you later persuaded him."

She gazed out the window. "I wanted to ask about the seriousness of his illness and what's being done to help him, but I was worried it would only discourage him."

"He does dialysis regularly, but the royal physician has been candid with my uncle. It is unlikely the king will last through winter. But then again, he didn't think he'd make it through autumn."

"He does seem very weak."

"But happy to see you." Anton turned down a narrow side street and parked. "My sister, Elsa, owns this restaurant. If you don't mind, we'll sneak in the back door."

"I don't mind at all."

"Elsa went to culinary school in Paris," he explained as he helped Adelaide out of the car. "Her French cuisine has become so popular, you need reservations to dine here—even for lunch."

"Even if you're her brother?" Adelaide teased.

"Unless you want to eat in the kitchen." He winked.

Elsa warmly greeted them, leading them to a corner table

nicely set for two, complete with a complimentary bottle of sauvignon blanc. Elsa poured them each a glass while she made several tempting suggestions for their meal. After their orders were placed, Adelaide surveyed the nearly full restaurant, taking in the white fairy lights and the evergreens draped from the timber beams.

"Your sister has already decorated for Christmas."

"Elsa adores this holiday and has barely begun." Anton took a sip of his wine. "She will keep adding her special touches over the next few days."

"Well, it's perfectly lovely."

For the next hour, they visited congenially over a delicious consommé and the most tender trout Adelaide had ever tasted. Their meal was followed with crème caramel and espresso. She'd never eaten food like this—delectable but not too heavy. She was also grateful that the conversation hadn't been heavy either. Anton kept things light and cheery, not saying a word about King Max, his health, or the challenges ahead.

"Would you like to stroll through the village?" he asked her as they exited, waving goodbye to Elsa.

"I'd love it. Not just to see everything but to walk off this lunch. I can't believe it's just a few hours until I'll be having dinner with the king."

"And the queen," he added quietly.

"Oh?"

"I didn't want to say anything, but it's one of the reasons I thought a good lunch might be important today."

"Meaning dinner might be unappetizing."

"Oh, the palace food is delightful." He grinned at her, and she got his meaning. They strolled in amiable silence for a few minutes before Anton stopped in front of a storefront. "Here is the chocolate shop my mum loves."

"Let's go in." Despite not being the least bit hungry, Adelaide was overwhelmed by the intoxicating smell in the shop. She got a few chocolates to save for later, as well as a similar selection to give to King Max.

"You might have to sneak those past the queen," Anton warned as they left.

She nodded. "Thanks for the heads-up."

As they continued strolling and visiting shops, Adelaide was surprised by how many people greeted Anton by name. Finally, they headed back to his SUV. "I thought you represented the Gruber province," she said, "and yet you know so many people here."

"I guess I get around." He chuckled. "But bear in mind, Montovia has a very small population. Plus, some folks here, like my sister, grew up in Gruber. I guess it's a small world after all." He actually started to hum the old tune with the same name.

She laughed. "You know that song?"

He nodded as he put his key in the ignition. "We may seem remote here, but we do have TV. And I used to visit my grandmother's house in Britain a lot when I was a small boy. I was always enthralled by her VHS player and collection of old movies."

"I guess it is a small world after all. Even so, I can't imagine living in a place where so many people know me by name. Even on campus, I feel mostly invisible."

"You wouldn't be invisible here." He smiled. "You might not have noticed, but you were getting a lot of stares."

"Because I'm a newcomer?"

"A very attractive newcomer."

She felt her cheeks warm.

"I apologize. I shouldn't have said that."

"No, no, it's okay. I'm just not used to flattery."

"Not flattery. Simply a sincere observation." He turned on the engine.

Wanting to switch topics, she asked about her palace tour.

Anton stole a glance at her as he pulled onto the street. "I haven't worn you out yet?"

"Well, I still have almost two hours before dinner. I'd love to see more of the palace. Besides, I'm afraid if I go to my room, I'll just crash onto that wonderful bed and not wake up until tomorrow. Can you imagine what the queen would think if I missed my first royal dinner?"

He shrugged. "Oh, I don't know. She might be glad."

At a loss for words once again, she cast her eyes down. "Speaking of the royal dinner," she said, rubbing her palms over her pants, "I'm worried I haven't brought the right clothes."

"The right clothes?"

"My law student wardrobe isn't exactly fit for royalty. Do you think the queen will mind? I mean, I might be having flashbacks to scenes in *Downton Abbey*, but I don't want to insult anyone by dressing too casually. I only own two skirts. Plain ones, like I wore today. To be honest, I live in blue jeans most of the time."

"I do too, when I'm not working."

"But really, how should I dress for dinner? What will the queen expect? I'd like to get off on the right foot with her."

He frowned. "Honestly?"

"Yes," she said, "honestly." She was surprised by her candidness with Anton but felt she could trust him.

"I'm no expert, but the women at palace dinners usually dress"—he gave her current outfit a once-over—"a bit more formally."

"Like gowns and jewels?" She grimaced.

"No, no. Not for a casual dinner. Maybe a skirt or dress. Not trousers. The queen is old-fashioned like that."

"Okay. I'll change back into my skirt."

He held up his index finger. "Although . . . there is a women's shop on the other end of town—my aunt's favorite. I believe the queen shops there. If you like, we could stop, and you could look around. We can save the palace tour for tomorrow."

She bit her lip. Her bank account was low on cash. She did have her emergency credit card, but this wasn't an emergency.

"I'm no fashion expert, Adelaide, but your concern about appearances is a valid one," he said. "After all, you are a princess. Knowing Queen Johanna, you can be certain she will critique your wardrobe. And I doubt she will offer assistance."

Adelaide considered this. Perhaps it was an emergency. She really didn't want to get on the queen's bad side the first time they met. If nothing else, she'd do it for the sake of King Max. She could imagine him jumping to her defense, and she hated to put him under more stress. "Yes, I think you're right. I'd like to visit that shop if you don't mind."

"Not at all."

Neither of them spoke as he turned the car in the opposite direction. When they arrived in town, finding a place to park proved difficult, so he stopped in the street and nodded toward a swanky-looking shop. "It's called Stilvoll," he said. "German for stylish."

"Just what I need." She heard her own sarcasm.

"Go ahead and look around while I park and make a phone call. I'll be in shortly."

Feeling very much like a fish out of water, Adelaide entered what appeared to be a very chic and expensive store. A well-dressed woman politely greeted her in German.

"Do you speak English?"

"Ja." She nodded eagerly. "You are not from here?"

"I'm an American, and I need a dress. Not a formal gown. Just a nice dress for a nice dinner. Do you have something like that?"

"Ja, ja, of course." She led her toward the back, indicating a rack of dresses of various styles, lengths, and fabrics. Adelaide peeked at a few of the tags, but the size numbers made no sense.

"Can you help me with sizes?" Adelaide asked.

The woman looked her up and down. "You are like my size, I think. Thirty-six or perhaps thirty-eight."

"Really?" Adelaide frowned. "That sounds too large."

"Thirty-six is American size eight."

"Oh." She nodded. "Okay."

The saleswoman pointed to a section on the rack, then peered intently at Adelaide. "Green is good on you? Good with your eyes."

"I do like green."

The woman removed a satiny dress and held it up. The front was too low-cut for Adelaide's taste, plus the fabric looked overly shiny. Not to mention the price was ridiculous. She shook her head as she reached for a dark green velveteen dress with a more conservative cut. Not showy, but somewhat sophisticated.

"No, no, that is for old frau," the woman said. "Not you."

"I like it." Adelaide also liked the price. "May I try it on?"

The woman shrugged, then led her to a changing room. While Adelaide was zipping it up, she overheard Anton speaking to the woman in German. They conversed too quickly for her to follow, but the woman sounded pleased. Very pleased. Because the changing room was small and poorly lit, Adelaide slipped out to peek into the better-lit mirror just outside the fitting room.

"Very nice," Anton said when he saw her.

"Really? It doesn't look like an old frau's dress?" She glanced at the saleswoman, who covered her mouth and giggled.

"Not on you." He came closer. "You look respectably stylish. Very suitable for a royal family dinner."

"Good." She felt relieved.

Now the saleswoman came over, cradling several more dresses in her arms. "You should try these too." She smiled. "Your size."

"No thanks. I like this one."

"But not just one." She held the dresses out toward Adelaide. "A princess needs more than just one."

Adelaide glanced nervously at Anton. "You told her that I'm—"

"It's all right. I called the palace and Herr Schneider actually

spoke with the king just now. Your father is eager for all to know
he has a daughter. He has authorized all your purchases, and he
encourages you to gather a suitable wardrobe for the upcoming
season's festivities. As it turns out, the royal family already has
an account here. You are to use it for anything you need." He
pointed to the saleswoman, who was beaming. She probably
worked on commission. "Frieda is happy to help. I've explained
to her what you'll need."

"But I—"

"It will please your father," he said quietly but firmly. "Now,
if you don't mind, I'll leave you ladies to it. I need to make a
few more phone calls." He glanced at his watch. "I'll be back
around five, if you don't mind."

"But I don't need—"

"Do it for your father," he insisted. "He rarely puts demands
on anyone, but Herr Schneider said he adamantly asked for
this."

She took in a deep breath, then nodded. "Fine, I will do my
best. For the king." She lowered her voice. "But for the record,
I'm in over my head here. I've never been good at this sort of
thing."

Anton patted Frieda's back. "That's why you have this expert
to help you." He looked at Frieda. "Do keep in mind that Frau
Smith is a princess, and she should dress in a manner befitting
a princess. Stylishly respectable."

Frieda nodded. "Ja. I do understand."

Anton smiled at Adelaide, tipped his head to both of them,
then made an overly eager exit.

Frieda went to work. Rather, Adelaide went to work. It
was a marathon of trying on many garments, shoes, boots,
and accessories. She couldn't recall how often she'd said ja or
nein, but by five, her green velveteen dress was in a garment
bag to take with her, as well as a pair of pretty black pumps
in a box. Everything else was scheduled for delivery to the

palace the next morning. She let Anton help her back into the Land Rover.

As he drove her the short distance to the palace, Adelaide was too exhausted to speak and, to her relief, he seemed to understand. She vaguely wondered how long she'd been awake by now. It felt like days. She suddenly envisioned herself dining with the king and queen, all prim and proper and cordial during the first course, but then falling dead asleep . . . and doing a face-plant right into the soup.

Seven

At exactly six o'clock, Adelaide, dressed in her new gown, made her way to the door that led to the royal family living area, just like Anton had told her to do. Taking a deep, calming breath, she rang the bell with a silent prayer for this evening to proceed smoothly.

A woman in a maid's uniform answered. "Welcome, Frau Smith. Please, come in." She led her into a cozy living room, which was more formal than Adelaide's taste and didn't really look like a room in a palace. "Please, sit."

Adelaide thanked her and sat in a wingback chair that faced the fireplace, which was warmly crackling. Relieved to have this moment alone to acclimate to this new setting, she leaned back and tried to relax by closing her eyes. But when she felt herself nearly falling asleep, she jerked herself awake.

It took a moment to get her bearings, but according to the ornate mantel clock, it was now 6:20. Had she gotten the time wrong? Or was this considered just being elegantly late? But wasn't that for guests, not hosts? Oh, how would she know?

"Hello?" A woman's voice made Adelaide jump—literally—to her feet. She turned to see a tall, dark-haired woman approaching from what she assumed was the private section of the royal home. Dressed in a midnight blue dress with several strands of pearls on the bodice, the woman looked elegantly austere. Like a smooth, deep lake on a cold winter's day.

"You must be Frau Smith. I am Queen Johanna." Adelaide noted that the queen's accent was thicker than her husband's. "Welcome to my home." She came over to take Adelaide's hand, but hers were so cold they sent a shiver through Adelaide. "Please, excuse my cool hands and my tardiness. I took a brisk stroll with the dogs, and the air turned to ice. I hoped for a warm bath, but our early dinner plans prohibited it."

"You should come over to the fire. It's nice and warm here." Adelaide noticed the queen's narrowed eyes and was reminded of her place. She was not the host and perhaps not even a truly welcomed guest. She had overstepped in inviting the queen to her own hearth.

"Max will be in shortly. He does not move too fast these days."

Adelaide glanced toward the door the queen just entered through to see it opening again. She watched a lanky, light-haired man enter the room. He gaped awkwardly in her direction, then turned his gaze to the queen with a crooked smile.

"Sorry to be late." He came over to Adelaide, looking on with open curiosity.

"Have you met my son, Prince Georg?" The queen seemed to hold her head even higher.

"No," Adelaide said. "I haven't had the pleasure."

"So, *you* are Adelaide." Georg clasped her hand. To her relief, his hand wasn't as icy as his mother's. "Pleasure to meet you. Are you enjoying Montovia?"

"Very much so." She forced a smile. "I spent some time in the village this afternoon. You have a beautiful home."

"Where did they put you?" he asked.

"Put me?"

"Your room. I assume you are on the second floor."

60

"My room is on this floor."

Georg's brows arched as he glanced at his mother.

"It's a lovely room," Adelaide said quickly, eager to gloss over whatever was happening. "The view from this floor is spectacular. I'm most appreciative."

"Hello!" a cheerful voice interrupted the tense interaction.

Adelaide turned toward the other end of the room where a different door was opening. King Max, in a wheelchair, was being guided in by Herr Schneider. Eager for a friendly face, she went over to greet him, taking both his hands in hers. "Good evening, King Max. I'm so happy to see you again."

His eyes gleamed. "Excuse my late entrance." He glanced at Herr Schneider. "It's his fault."

Herr Schneider simply nodded.

"He insisted I needed to shave." He rubbed his chin. "Perhaps I did."

"Are you joining us for dinner, Herr Schneider?" the queen asked a bit sharply.

He politely declined. As he excused himself, Adelaide stepped behind the wheelchair. "Would you like to sit by the fire?" she asked the king. "It's quite nice."

"Danke, mein lieber, danke schoen!" He thanked her profusely as she wheeled him past his wife and stepson, both of whom watched on with curious expressions. "Are you quite comfortable here? Und in your room?"

"Oh, yes. I was just telling Queen Johanna and Prince Georg what a beautiful home you have. My suite is perfectly lovely." She waved her hand before her. "And this one is too. Someone has a very good eye for interior decor." She glanced at the queen. "Is that your responsibility?"

"I do what I can," she said stiffly.

"The queen's decorator is always changing something," the king said with what sounded like disdain. "I can get lost in my own home."

"Let's proceed to the dining room," the queen announced and, nudging Adelaide out of the way, waved to her son. "Prince Georg will help his father to the table."

"Yes, of course." Adelaide stepped aside, watching Georg fumble to manipulate the wheelchair through the dining room entry.

"You sit there." The queen pointed to the long side of the fully set rectangular table. And as she unceremoniously took a chair at one end, Georg wheeled the king opposite her. As he took the chair across from Adelaide, he grinned at her as if he'd just suppressed a good joke. The queen rang a brass bell, and a uniformed maid emerged with a tray of soup dishes.

The soup was good, with no face-plants executed, but it was nothing like the consommé she'd enjoyed at lunch. King Max seemed extra quiet as he ate, but Adelaide noticed him watching everyone like an old hawk. Queen Johanna attempted polite but disinterested conversation with Adelaide until her son took over.

"What is your life like in America?" Georg asked.

She told him a bit about the university she attended and the demands of law school.

Georg's brows arched. "You study law?"

"I hope to graduate next year and take my boards so I can begin my practice."

"Back in America?" the queen queried.

"Yes, of course."

"You could practice law here," King Max said. "You could start next week if you like."

"Really? Just like that?" Adelaide didn't know much about Montovian law, but was it that simple to start a law practice?

"If I say so." He set his spoon in the bowl with a clang.

Georg looked skeptical. "A woman attorney in Montovia?"

"Why not?" the king shot back. "We have women doctors."

"Does she even know our laws?" Georg asked.

Adelaide tried to think of a way to segue this conversation. "How about you, Prince Georg? Tell me about your education. What are your interests?"

King Max huffed but said nothing.

"I have not pursued university education," Georg told her.

"Prince Georg is privately tutored by Prime Minister Kovacs," Queen Johanna said. "That is an education for leadership and far more suited to a member of the royal family."

King Max cleared his throat. "And when were you last tutored by Albert?" He directed his question to Georg.

"You know Georg only just returned from his Swiss ski holiday two days ago," Queen Johanna said to her husband. "Now that he's rested, I need his help. He will supervise the Christmas decorations."

King Max scowled but kept his peace.

Adelaide hoped to detour to a more pleasant conversation. "What sort of decorations?"

"The palace Christmas decorations are elaborate and extensive," Queen Johanna told her as the maid picked up the empty soup bowls. "We usually start sooner, but I have had other business. There is a crew coming tomorrow."

"The queen's crew will deck the halls from top to bottom," King Max told Adelaide in a tone that suggested disapproval.

"As did your mother," the queen sharply reminded him.

"Not the same way. Not to the degree you take it."

Adelaide didn't like where this was headed. "If you need any help, Queen Johanna, I'd be happy to step—"

"Thank you very much," the queen cut off her offer. "Prince Georg knows what I like and how I like it."

"I'd like your help, but my mother is *very* particular," Georg said with a wink.

As the maid returned with their entrées, Georg continued to tell Adelaide about his mother's superb Christmas decorations and how everyone in the kingdom loved them. "They come from all over to visit the palace and admire the decorations. I think we used half a million lights last year."

"Half a million?" King Max looked aghast. "You cannot be serious."

"It's true," Georg replied. "I counted them."

"One by one?" Adelaide leaned back as the maid set her entrée down.

"Nein." Georg winked. "By strand and by calculator."

"It must be spectacular." Adelaide could see by King Max's expression that he did not approve of this extravagance. She didn't either. Not that it was her business.

The king cleared his throat as he reached for his fork. "Since Georg is so occupied with decorating, perhaps Adelaide should meet with Albert in his place."

"Why should she do that?" the queen asked.

Ignoring his wife, the king turned to Adelaide. "It is an excellent idea. Albert will tutor you on our legal system. Would you like that?"

"I would love it! When I excused myself from my December exams, I assured my supervising professor that my trip here would be educational."

"And so it shall." King Max looked highly pleased with his suggestion, but the queen was glowering. Meanwhile, Georg seemed oblivious. He was watching Adelaide so attentively, she suspected he did not view her as a stepsister.

"We will meet in my private quarters tomorrow morning," the king told Adelaide. "You and Albert and me. We will all work together."

Queen Johanna slammed her fist down so firmly her wineglass jumped. "You cannot do that, Max. You are ill."

"I am feeling quite well. Princess Adelaide is good medicine. Even the nurse agreed I looked much better after her visit."

The queen said nothing, but she was obviously vexed. Once again, Adelaide felt the need to introduce a safer conversation topic, so she directed a question to Georg. "Where in Switzerland do you ski?"

Georg wiped his mouth with a napkin before answering. "Zermatt is the best."

"And what makes Zermatt the best?" she asked as if she had a clue to what she was talking about. But a good lawyer knows when to bluff.

"So many things. The people. The slopes. Do you know Zermatt?"

"No. I haven't had the pleasure."

"You can see Matterhorn from the resort."

"Oh, that does sound nice."

"Do you ski?" Georg asked eagerly.

"No. That's considered a rich person's sport where I live."

King Max cleared his throat. "It is a rich person's sport here too."

Adelaide suppressed a weary sigh. It seemed no matter the topic, things always rounded back to these troubled barbs. Clearly, the royal family was not a happy one. She vaguely wondered what it would've been like if her grandfather had allowed her birth parents to wed. Perhaps it would've been worse.

After dinner, the four of them visited briefly, and at times tersely, in the living room. But King Max was wearing out, and the queen sent a message to Herr Schneider to help him to his suite.

"I will see you in the morning," he told Adelaide. "Ten o'clock in my chambers."

"I'll be there." She reached for his hand. "Thank you, King Max, for your kind hospitality."

His smile warmed her. "You are most humbly welcome, but please, can you disperse with King Max and call me Father?"

She pursed her lips, then nodded. "I will try tomorrow."

He squeezed her fingers. "Thank you, mein lieber. Until tomorrow."

As he was wheeled away, Adelaide turned to her hostess. "Thank you, too, Queen Johanna, for your hospitality. I hope you will excuse—"

"No, no," Georg protested, "it is early yet."

"But I am—"

"We will have coffee," he insisted. "I want to know more about you. You are my first real American girl. Do not say good night so soon."

"I'm sorry, but I flew through the night and arrived this morning. I'm so sleepy I can barely keep my eyes open."

"Let her go," the queen told her son abruptly. "Can't you see she's tired?"

"Only if you promise to spend time with me later," Georg said. "You fascinate me. I need to know you more."

"Fine. I promise more time," she said. Anything to get out of here. "I apologize, but if I don't leave now, I might fall asleep on my feet."

"I won't let that happen." Georg hurried over to take her arm. "I will escort you safely to your room."

Queen Johanna said something to her son in German. The meaning slipped past Adelaide, but the tone was clear. She was not pleased by Georg's behavior. For that matter, Adelaide wasn't either.

"Thank you, but I can make it on my own." She pulled her arm away.

"I'll get you there," he declared.

Feeling too weary to argue, and worried the scowling queen was about to say "off with her head," Adelaide allowed Georg to escort her, but when he lingered by her door, she firmly disengaged her arm from his, told him a crisp "gute nacht," then went into her room and locked the door. As she kicked off her shoes, she wondered what on earth she had done to encourage the prince and what she could do to get him to back off. She would have to think about that in the morning.

Eight

A delaide had never slumbered in such a comfortable bed, luxurious room, or peaceful place, but she still woke up at the crack of dawn the next morning. She refused to allow herself to calculate exactly what time it would be in Virginia. She'd heard her phone ping in the middle of the night but had ignored it. Looking now, she saw that Maya had tried checking up on her. Even though Adelaide knew it was the middle of the night back home, she texted her friend back anyway. Just to remind her of the time difference and let her know that everything was okay. At least, she hoped so.

Adelaide took her time getting ready for the day, vaguely wondering what she should do about breakfast. It wasn't that she was hungry, but coffee did sound good. She was about to go exploring when her phone pinged again. This time it was Anton, politely inquiring about today's schedule and wondering if she would still like the full palace tour. She texted back saying she was on board as long as the tour included coffee. His response was immediate. He told her to meet him on the second floor.

When she got there, Anton was already waiting for her. He

led her through a generous dining room to a kitchen where someone had set out a continental breakfast with coffee and tea. As they dined on pastries, cheese, fruit, and coffee, she told him a bit about the previous night's royal dinner.

"I didn't expect the queen to give you a warm reception." He whispered although no one was around to hear him.

"Prince Georg made up for that." She tore apart a flaky croissant and chuckled. "That guy has a lot of nerve."

"What did he do?" Anton's brows drew together.

"Oh, nothing, really. He just seems to assume I am his new best friend."

"Interesting." Anton looked amused.

She frowned. "Isn't it kind of creepy? We're sort of like step-siblings."

"Of no relation. Prince Georg may see you as a way to secure the throne."

She wrinkled her nose at him. "Well, that's flattering."

"I'm sure he also noticed your many fine qualities." He smirked back at her. "Sorry. To be honest, I'm not surprised to hear of the prince's interest."

"Hello there."

They both looked up as an older gentleman entered the room. He waved and smiled. Anton stood and introduced him as Prime Minister Albert Kovacs. "My esteemed uncle."

"I'm happy to meet you." Adelaide shook his hand. "You look almost as I imagined."

He held her hand, looking deeply into her eyes. "You are more lovely than I imagined. A pleasing combination of your father—and your mother."

Her spirits dipped at the mention of her mother. She pulled her hand back as she looked down.

"Did I offend you?"

"This is the third anniversary of her mother's tragic accident," Anton quietly told his uncle.

"Ja, I am so sorry." Albert put a comforting arm around her shoulders. "Losing a mother is difficult. More so if you are young. I am so very sorry."

She met his gaze. "Thank you."

"Hopefully we can distract you with more pleasant things," Anton told her.

"Ja. I hear you are my new pupil," Albert said.

Anton looked at her. "What is this?"

"The king has arranged it to help me understand Montovian law," she explained. "I'm very eager to learn."

"Is it something I can sit in on too?" Anton asked his uncle.

"I see no reason you cannot join us. We meet at ten o'clock. I'll see you both in the king's quarters following a short meeting with the royal council." Albert checked his watch. "You'll have to excuse me, Princess. I'm due there now."

She nodded.

"And we're due to take a tour of the palace," Anton said.

For the next hour, he gave her the full tour—including the dark, musty dungeons, which were mostly used for storage. Finally they headed clear up to the highest turret, above the roofline, where they took their second cups of coffee and sat down to enjoy the amazing view of the surrounding countryside.

"You sure know your way around the palace," she said as she gazed out over the mist-draped hills.

"I've been coming here with my uncle since I was a boy. When left to my own devices, I would slip away and explore to my heart's content."

"What a fun way to grow up." She felt a surprising rush of envy.

"No complaints." He peered curiously at her. "What was your childhood like?"

She had no desire to speak about her lackluster and somewhat underprivileged childhood. At least, underprivileged by palace standards. Not because she was ashamed, but out of respect for her mother. Especially today. "My childhood was fine. Very different from this. But just fine." She didn't mean to sound snippy, but she noticed his eyes flicker with concern.

Without missing a beat, he wisely changed the topic. "I'm impressed by your interest in Montovian law."

"Well, I am studying law in the States." She tried to brighten her tone. "And I do love to learn. I'm honored the king and your uncle are willing to meet with me."

He took a swig from his coffee mug. "I'm honored too. They both have a wealth of information. My degree was political science, but the best education is from real life." His phone alarm dinged. "Time to go meet them."

On their way to the king's chambers, Adelaide noticed Prince Georg rounding a corner with a large box in his hands. She tried to continue unnoticed, but it was too late.

"There you are." Prince Georg hurried to catch them. "My favorite princess. Good morning."

She smiled politely despite the urge to run in the opposite direction. "Getting ready to help with decorations? That seems like a fun job."

"It would be more fun if you helped." He beamed at her.

"Sorry. We have a meeting." She nodded to Anton.

"And we don't want to be late." Anton nudged her along.

"I will be in the main hall," Georg called after them. "Come join me when your meeting is done, Princess Adelaide."

"Later," she called back as Anton escorted her down another hallway.

"He certainly is persistent," Anton said when they were out of earshot.

"So it seems."

The king grew weary after only an hour of discussing Montovian law, so he excused himself for a little rest, but not before he invited Adelaide to meet up with him for lunch at one.

"He seems so frail," Adelaide said after Herr Schneider wheeled the king away.

"He is more energetic now that you are here," Albert told her.

Adelaide cringed to imagine how worn out he must've been —maybe he still was but was trying to conceal it. "Has the king had the best medical help available? I'm no expert, but I know cancer research and new procedures are constantly improving. Does he have access to the most modern—"

"Our hospital and medical staff are quite modern," Albert said, sounding defensive.

Adelaide backpedaled. "I didn't mean to suggest they weren't."

"A renowned Swiss oncologist has been treating him," Anton said.

"Right." She nodded glumly. "I guess—I just wish . . . I mean, I barely know him. I'd hate to lose him."

Albert let out a long sigh. "Unfortunately, his liver trouble is congenital. It is the same thing his father suffered with at about the king's age. The prognosis is not good. To be honest, I worried he would be gone before your arrival. I do not like to bear bad news, but the oncologist told me only yesterday that he doubts the king will last until Christmas."

She felt a lump in her throat. "I understand."

"Perhaps we've covered enough law for the first day." Albert slid a book across the table to her. "Much of what we discussed this morning is in this book. Perhaps you would like to take it with you. Our laws are not complicated, but they are different from the United States."

"Yes. Thank you." She felt overwhelmed as she picked up the book. Not about Montovian law but, instead, the impending loss of the father she had barely started to know. "If you will, please excuse me."

The men stood and Albert rested a comforting hand on her shoulder. "I know this is hard on you, Adelaide. A lot to take in."

She just nodded.

Albert tipped his head to his nephew. "Anton has volunteered to be at your disposal for the duration of your visit." His countenance brightened slightly. "I hope it will be a lengthy one."

She thanked him, then excused herself again, barely making it out of the meeting room before tears came tumbling down. Unaccustomed to so much emotion, and embarrassed by it, she hurried to her suite. She could blame her feelings on tiredness or her mother's anniversary, but she knew this was about the king—the father she would never get the chance to fully know. She allowed herself a brief cry, then splashed cold water on her face and took the book Albert had given her to the cozy chair by the window. Studying was something she was good at, something she could control.

For the next hour, determined to prove herself as an intelligent, worthy daughter, she pored over the lawbook until it was time to join the king for lunch. As she walked to the dining area, she prepared herself for another awkward encounter with the queen and prince but was relieved to discover this meal was just her and the king.

The two visited comfortably as they ate. She asked lots of questions about the kingdom and about some of the things she'd read. He asked about her life, her dreams, and her impressions of the kingdom. Two hours passed quickly, and soon Herr Schneider, as well as the king's nurse, insisted King Max needed to rest. Although Adelaide was reluctant to part ways, she didn't want to overtax the king.

"You will come for dinner again?" he asked as she prepared to go. "At six o'clock?"

Although she didn't relish another dinner like last night, for the king's sake, she agreed. On her way to her suite, she was literally cornered by Prince Georg. "Aha, I have been looking for you," he said. "I need your help with something."

She pointed to herself. "My help?"

"Yes. I need a female opinion on a decoration decision, and my mother is away until dinnertime."

She shrugged. "Okay. What can I help you with?"

"Come to the first floor with me." He led her to the elevator, chattering in a friendly manner all the way down. First, he showed her what had already been done in the entry hall. Strings of white lights and garlands with golden ribbons hung from every available surface. Fancy metallic ornaments adorned everything, looking expensive and elaborate and, in her opinion, a bit over the top. But then, she reminded herself, this was a palace.

She took a second to choose her words wisely. "It's very nice."

"Yes, I think so too."

She pointed to the enormous evergreen tree that had been set in place. Although completely bare, it was majestic just the same. "What a handsome tree."

"Yes, that is why I wanted your opinion. Mother got new gold and silver ornaments from a catalog last summer. They were very expensive and, as you observed in the entry hall, quite impressive, but there is disagreement over what to use."

He led her to a seasonal storage room where labeled boxes were arranged on shelves and a large worktable was strewn with miscellaneous decorations. "In the past, we always used these red velvet ribbons and the more traditional baubles." He hung a rocking horse ornament from his little finger.

"Cute." Adelaide picked up a faux gingerbread man, letting it spin on its string. "This is adorable." She reached for a grinning elf decoration and smiled. "So is this."

"Mother feels they are too old-fashioned, but the head chef complained over this new direction." He picked up a golden ball bedecked with faux jewels. "Chef Braun says we are mistaken to use such ornate decorations on the tree. And the head housekeeper says children will be disappointed." He picked up a string of multicolored lights. "We always used these, but Mother wants white lights. She wants the tree to match the splendor of the rest of the hall. Now I am unsure."

"I see." Adelaide fingered a colorful string of faux candies, thinking how appealing it would be to young children. "I think these old-fashioned decorations are delightful."

"Really? Better than these?" He waved to an unopened box of glass ornaments that shimmered like gold.

She shrugged. "You asked for my opinion. All I can say is, I agree with the head chef and housekeeper. I think the old decorations are perfectly charming. No wonder the children love them. I'm not a child, but I love them too."

He nodded. "Then we do it the old way. As soon as my work crew returns." He went to work finding old boxes of ornaments and putting the new boxes back on a shelf. Meanwhile, curious about the many boxes of decorations, Adelaide began to poke around the room. Seeing a stack of dusty boxes tucked in a corner, all labeled the same, she grew curious. "Weihnachtskrippe?" she read the word aloud. "What does that mean?"

"Those are just the old figures for the nativity scene."

"Oh?" She opened a box, carefully peeling back layers of worn tissue paper to reveal a large carved figurine of a shepherd with a lamb under one arm. "Oh, how beautiful," she said with enthusiasm. She lifted the shepherd from the box. "Where will the nativity go?"

Georg shrugged as he set another bin of multicolored lights on the table. "Mother doesn't care for it. She does not display the Weihnachtskrippe anymore."

"Oh?" She tucked the shepherd back in his place and replaced the cover. "That's a shame. And such fine craftsmanship too."

More workers entered the storage room. With Prince Georg

busy assigning tasks, Adelaide slipped out unnoticed. She was just heading up the stairs when her phone pinged. A text from Anton invited her for tea. She eagerly accepted. To her pleasant surprise, he was still at the palace.

As she hurriedly gathered her coat to meet him downstairs, she wondered if her enthusiasm was to escape the palace for a spell or because she was becoming quite fond of Anton. But she reminded herself, there was no point in becoming romantically involved. After Christmas break, or as soon as the king passed, whichever came first, she would be returning to America.

CHAPTER

Nine

After a pleasant afternoon tea, Anton and Adelaide
took a stroll through the village. It was growing even
more festive with strings of lights framing windows,
evergreen wreaths on doors, and the occasional nativity scene
displayed in shop fronts. They returned to the palace in the
early evening, and Adelaide prepared herself for another awkward dinner with the royal family. She knew this was the plan
because someone had slipped a schedule under the door of
her bedroom suite. As Adelaide put on a simple black frock
accented by a silver cross necklace her mother had given her
years ago, she suspected Queen Johanna was behind the rather
packed schedule.

The queen probably wanted to keep Adelaide away from
the king's company during her visit. But a quick phone call to
Anton confirmed that Adelaide's time was hers to spend as she
pleased, and the most important time spent, Anton and Albert
agreed, was with her father.

Feeling only somewhat relieved, Adelaide forced a smile when
Queen Johanna welcomed her into the royal living room at six.
Prince Georg was already there, standing by the fireplace, and

King Max was just being rolled in. Greetings were exchanged and hors d'oeuvres were consumed, but after they were seated in the dining room, it grew clear that the queen was even more agitated than she had been the previous night.

"Tomorrow is December the first. Our busy time of year." She directed her words to Adelaide. "I assume you saw the agenda my private secretary prepared for you."

"Yes, thank you. I'll keep your suggestions in mind," Adelaide said pleasantly. "Although I'm sure you're aware my highest priority is time with King Max."

"Now, now." The king held up one hand. "Adelaide, didn't you promise to stop calling me King Max?"

"Oh?" Adelaide glanced at the queen, whose well-shaped brows were so closely drawn that two sharp creases lay etched between them.

"I *am* your father," the king continued. "It would give me great pleasure to hear my daughter address me as such."

"Yes, I'll try to remember that," Adelaide said quietly.

The queen's expression grew even darker as she forked a green bean hostilely. Georg seemed oblivious to the drama, or perhaps just more interested in roast beef than family feuding.

"Do you know tomorrow is the first day of Montovia's Christmas festivities?" the king asked Adelaide.

"Yes. I was in the village this afternoon, admiring all the shops' wonderful decorations." She kept her voice cheery. "I was trying to imagine how sweet it will all look with snow. Just like a Christmas card."

"I hear we will have snow by next week," the king told her.

"Speaking of decorations," the queen said, sliding into the conversation, "I understand Adelaide has recommended a change in my plans for the main hall."

"How good of you to get involved," the king said to Adelaide.

"I do not think it good," the queen retorted.

Adelaide glanced at Georg. "I only gave Prince Georg my opinion." She hoped the prince might clarify, but when he didn't, she continued. "He asked what I thought of your new decorations, and I—"

"*New* decorations?" King Max stared at his wife. "What's this?"

"I'm sure I told you," she said smoothly. "The old decorations looked so tattered and worn. Not befitting a palace. I ordered new ones months ago."

King Max frowned, then turned to Adelaide. "So, tell me, mein lieber, what did you think of the queen's *new* decorations?"

Adelaide considered her words before speaking. "Well, they're quite grand. Very regal. But I'm not a fancy person. I prefer gingerbread figures to jeweled, golden harps."

To Adelaide's relief, Georg jumped in, explaining how the palace staff had complained about the overly fancy decorations. "So, we put up the tree just like it's always been." He reached for his phone and started pulling up photos to show the king. "See, this is a picture of Mother's new decorations. Very glamorous, indeed." He swiped his finger across the screen. "And here is the tree with the old decorations."

"I agree with Adelaide," King Max declared. "All that gold and glitz is pretentious. I prefer our traditional decorations. Reminds me of my boyhood. Old-fashioned and friendly."

The queen set down her water goblet with a thud. "But this is a palace, Max. We live in modern times. The decor should reflect that kind of sophistication."

King Max let out a weary sigh but said nothing. Meanwhile, the queen scowled.

"Your decorations are very elegant, Mother." Georg sounded apologetic.

"Oh, yes," Adelaide jumped in. "Very sophisticated."

King Max frowned but remained quiet. Perhaps too tired to engage.

"It's not my place to question," Adelaide began carefully, "but is the main hall tree meant to be for the enjoyment of the royal family or for the citizens of Montovia?"

King Max answered slowly, "Historically, and not so long ago, the main hall decorations were for villagers. The king would send the invitation to all, welcoming them to the palace for the start of Advent. And then sometimes again for a Saint Nicholas Day celebration. There would be music and fun. Villagers would be served gingerbread and Vanillekipferl cookies and mulled wine. Happy times." With a faraway look in his eyes, he sighed. "I suppose I am old-fashioned, but I remember those times with happiness."

"Maybe it's better to keep the traditional decorations down there in the main hall," Adelaide suggested, "and reserve the fancy golden ones for the spaces occupied by the royal family up here. The royal quarters could be elegantly decorated."

"I agree with the first part of your recommendation," King Max told her. "But must I tolerate pretentious bejeweled ornaments in my own living space when I, like you, would prefer gingerbread and candy canes?"

Queen Johanna's silence was frosty. Her eyes were like fiery arrows, aimed directly at Adelaide. And yet Adelaide was still not willing to back down. For her father's sake, she would speak up.

"You are the king, are you not?" she challenged him. "If you don't want fancy decorations in your palace or personal home, you should not be subjected to them."

King Max actually chuckled. "Spoken like a true princess."

"I suppose you would like me to throw all my decorations in the rubbish?" The queen crossed her arms.

"Or give them to the poor. Although perhaps the poor would not like them either." King Max grinned at Adelaide. "What do you think?"

Adelaide, not eager to stir up more controversy, decided to

switch topics. "I just remembered the beautiful nativity set I spied in the holiday storage room. It appears hand-carved and rather old. I'm curious as to the story behind it." She rested her hand on the king's. "Father, why don't you care to use it during Christmas?"

"Oh, ja, the Weihnachtskrippe." He rubbed a wrinkled hand over his chin. "I have not seen it in years. Is it still down there?"

"Well, I only saw the shepherd piece, but there were certainly a lot of boxes down there. All marked 'Weihnachtskrippe.'"

"My great-grandmother commissioned a very talented wood carver to make that set about a hundred years ago. My mother told me about it when I was a boy. It took the old wood-carver three years to complete it, and he was so old when he started, they did not know if he'd live to finish it. I always loved those pieces. Each one is a true work of art. I used to help my mother set up the Weihnachtskrippe in the main hall. Always to the left of the staircase, opposite the big tree. We'd place real straw in the stable and manger. With good lighting, it was quite magnificent and rather realistic. The children always loved it."

"It sounds delightful." Adelaide smiled.

The king turned to his wife. "Why has the Weihnachtskrippe not been used?" But before she could answer, he turned back to Adelaide. "I assign that task to you, mein lieber. Will you arrange the Weihnachtskrippe for me?"

"I would be honored, Father."

"Christmas is about the babe in the manger," he said solemnly. "We need not forget that. Can you do it tomorrow, Adelaide? For the start of Advent?"

"I'd love to." Adelaide fingered her silver cross. "Because I agree, Father. The babe in the manger is why we celebrate Christmas. To honor him."

His eyes glistened as he beamed at her. Was it because she'd supported his views or because she'd started to call him Father? Perhaps both. But it warmed her from head to toe, helping to defrost the queen's cold vibes that chilled her to the bone.

As Georg enthusiastically offered to help Adelaide with the nativity project, Queen Johanna remained quiet, a smoldering silence that Adelaide felt responsible for. Although she regretted causing this disharmony within the royal family, she did not regret standing by her father. If the queen wanted a showdown, she might've met her match in Adelaide. But hopefully not in front of the king.

To Adelaide's dismay, Georg made good on his offer to help with the nativity the next day. But she took charge by tasking him with the transport of the boxes and heavy wooden platform to the hall. Naturally, he delegated this chore to someone else. The same thing happened when she asked him to find some hay and the needed lighting. After she had everything necessary, Georg sat nearby, watching from a chair and chattering at her as she arranged and rearranged the pieces until she felt it was all perfect.

"So beautiful," she said more to herself than Georg.

"Yes . . . *very*." Georg's whisper was so close behind her, she imagined his breath on the back of her neck. She cringed and stepped away, pulling out her phone.

"I want pictures." She moved away from Georg. "To show the king."

"You did a good job with it." Georg kept his eyes on her as she took shots from various angles, zooming in on the Christ child in the manger. "Too bad Mother will hate it." He chuckled like this was humorous.

She pocketed her phone. "Yes, it is too bad." She pointed to the stack of empty boxes. "I'm sure you'll see that those get put away. I have an eleven o'clock appointment." Before he could respond, she took off running up the stairs. Georg wasn't a bad guy but his overly keen interest made her skin crawl.

She headed straight to the king's private quarters but was met outside his door by Queen Johanna.

"The king is not feeling well this morning," the queen informed her.

"I'm sorry to hear that." Adelaide glanced past her to the closed door. "Perhaps a little visit will improve his—"

"Do you *not* get my meaning?"

"I have an appointment with my father," Adelaide declared.

"Your appointment is canceled." Blocking the door, the queen crossed her arms in front of her.

"Then I will simply tell him good morning, wish him well, and be on my way." Adelaide reached past her royal roadblock for the doorbell, but the queen swatted her hand aside.

"Excuse me?" Adelaide stared into the icy blue eyes, then, without another word, elbowed past the rude woman to ring the doorbell. If Queen Johanna thought Adelaide a pushover, she had another think coming.

"Frau Smith." Herr Schneider sounded glad to see her.

"Is Father well enough for my visit?" She was still partly hidden by the queen.

"Yes." He opened the door wider, peering curiously at both of them. "Your father eagerly awaits your arrival, Princess Adelaide."

She smiled stiffly at the queen. "Seems you are confused. My father *is* expecting me." She gently but firmly pushed past the queen. "Please, excuse me."

"Mein leiber!" the king called from his chair. "My sunshine has arrived."

As she hurried to his side, she could see the queen still peering into the room as Herr Schneider closed the door. "Good morning, Father."

The king beamed at her. "Thank you for calling me Father. It does my old heart good."

She leaned over to kiss his cheek. "Thank *you* for allowing me to call you Father." She sat across from him and started describing her busy morning in the great hall. "It's the most beautiful nativity I've ever seen. Each piece is so wonderfully carved and painted so delicately. It's so lifelike. I even chatted with some of the shepherds and angels."

He laughed, clapping his hands. "I knew you were the right one to take care of that for me. Danke schoen, mein lieber. I wish I could see it."

"Do you ever go down there?" she asked.

"Nein. My good doctor and nurse and Herr Schneider keep me locked up here like a prisoner."

Herr Schneider, who stood by the door, cleared his throat.

"A well-cared-for prisoner," Adelaide said. "They just want you to be well, Father. And I have a surprise." She pulled out her phone and showed him the photos of the finished nativity scene.

His eyes lit up. "It is perfect, mein lieber. Your grandmother Adelaide would be proud."

As they visited, she found she was doing most of the talking. It did seem his energy was less than yesterday, and she suspected he was trying hard to pretend it wasn't. Maybe the queen had been right . . .

"Queen Johanna thought you were not well enough for a visit," she told him. "I don't want to wear you out."

"Your visit breathes life into these old bones."

Now, in the hope of keeping him quiet, Adelaide told him about the last section of the Montovian lawbook she'd been reading. She asked a few questions, making sure they could be easily answered with a word or two. She could see he was tired, but even more concerning was the tone of his skin. It seemed even more sallow today.

After an hour, the nurse came in with a tray laden with a

light lunch and some medicines. "I think this is my cue to go," she whispered. Standing up, she kissed him on the cheek again, then said "adieu."

He reached for her hand. "First you must promise to join me for dinner." He squeezed her fingers. "We will dine early so you can attend the festivities in the village."

"Oh, yes, tonight is the tree-lighting ceremony, isn't it?"

"Ja." He stuck out his bottom lip. "I am sorry to miss it, but my doctor has forbade me."

Hoping to distract him, she returned the conversation to the dinner plans. "You said an *early* dinner. What time shall I come?"

"Fünf." He held up a hand with fingers splayed and then switched to only two fingers. "For dinner only wir zwei. *We two.* Und we will eat in here."

"Oh?" Getting his meaning, she nodded eagerly. Just the two of them for dinner at five in his private quarters. "I look forward to it." As she left, her steps lightened at the thought of being spared from the rest of the royal family for one evening. Just the two of them. How lovely!

CHAPTER

CHAPTER

Ten

Dining alone with her father was much more enjoyable than with the royal family. Although she knew the queen would not approve, Adelaide was glad her father had planned it like this. He seemed to enjoy the more informal meal too.

"Everything was excellent," she proclaimed as a servant removed the last of the dishes.

The king set his napkin on the table. "I asked for all my favorite foods tonight."

"And it was all delicious. I've never eaten goose before—and that apple dressing was fabulous." She sipped her coffee. "What was that chocolate dessert called again?"

"Sacher torte." He leaned back with a satisfied smile. "I am not sad to miss the tree-lighting celebration, mein lieber."

"Why is that?"

"It will be cold . . . my old bones want the warm hearth."

"Then I'm glad you're not going." Yet she felt the stiffness in her smile. "I'll try to get some photos to bring back for you."

"Ja, ja, that will be good. But there is another reason I am not so sad, liebe Tochter."

She felt warmed to hear him call her *dear daughter*. "What is that, Father?"

"You must take my place."

"Take your place?"

"Ja. You will light the village tree tonight. Albert is informed of my plan. He will make your introduction."

"Really?" She blinked. "How exciting."

His eyes twinkled. "Ja, you will be well-received. It will be good."

She wasn't so sure she'd be well-received by all, primarily the queen, but not wanting to worry him, Adelaide kept her concerns to herself.

"You must dress for the cold."

"Yes." She nodded. "Anton said that snow is forecasted."

Her father called out to his ever-present assistant in fast German, asking him to fetch something. Adelaide couldn't make out what he had requested, but Herr Schneider took off like a shot.

"You are my representation," the king told her. "I cannot be present, but you will be like my . . ." His brow creased as if he were struggling for words. "My ambassador."

Herr Schneider returned to the room with a large rectangular box.

"Ja, ja." The king gestured for him to open it.

Herr Schneider did so, then peeled back layers of tissue paper to reveal a furry garment. The king instructed his aide to take out the dark brown coat and help Adelaide try it on.

Shocked by what she knew must be a very expensive coat made from real fur, and slightly worried about how some of her animal activist friends back home might react, she gingerly slipped her arms into it. The satin lining slid on easily, sumptuously. "Oh my." She didn't know what to say. "What is this made of?"

"Russian sable."

Although she wasn't sure what that meant, she suspected it was special by his tone.

"It belonged to my mother." His eyes twinkled as he looked at her. "A gift from my father for their twenty-fifth anniversary."

She stroked the soft fur. "It's beautiful."

"Beautiful like you, mein lieber Tochter. You must wear it with pride."

Adelaide wasn't sure about that, but holding her head high, she reminded herself that she would be representing the king tonight. "I will take good care of my grandmother's beautiful coat," she promised.

"It has been remade for you, Adelaide. It is *your* coat now." He reached for a blue box that had been tucked beneath his chair. "And you must also wear this." He handed her the velvet-covered box.

Almost afraid to breathe, she slowly opened it. "Oh, Father." She blinked at the sparkling necklace, then snapped the box closed again. "That is far too grand for me."

"Nonsense." He waved a hand at her. "The diamond necklace belonged to your grandmother. Your namesake. It is fitting you wear it tonight. And at other Christmas celebrations. You are a princess, Adelaide. I want you to look like one." His eyes looked misty. "It pleases me."

"I will wear it for you, Father."

"Danke schoen." He pointed to the mantel clock. "You must prepare yourself for the tree lighting. Anton will be waiting."

She kissed his cheek, thanking him again, and told herself she would return his lavish gifts before leaving for home. But for now, she would do what she could to make him proud and happy.

A driver dropped Adelaide and Anton off next to the village square, where crowds were already gathered around musicians and food kiosks. A tall evergreen was situated in the center of the square. "What a beautiful setting," Adelaide said. "The only thing missing is the snow."

"I just heard the weather forecast has put snow a few more days out."

"Well, it's still lovely." She smiled at a pair of cherub-like children waiting in line for a treat.

"And you are lovely too." Anton held out his arm. "Like a real princess."

More like a real Cinderella, she thought as she looped her arm through his. She'd already confessed to Anton how awkward she felt in furs and jewels. "I just hope I make the king proud," she murmured as he led her toward a platform where Albert and several other dignified-looking citizens were seated.

"You're to sit next to my uncle," Anton explained.

"What about you?"

"I'll be down here with the riffraff," he joked, pointing to the end of the table.

"Willkommen, Princess Adelaide." Albert stood to greet her. He shook her hand and pulled out a chair for her in the center of the long table. Then, taking his time, he politely introduced her to the others at the table, explaining who they were before he sat back down.

"Almost time." As Albert checked his watch, Adelaide noticed Queen Johanna and Georg walking through the growing crowd. Both held their heads high as they smiled and nodded as various greetings were tossed their way. Clearly they were used to being treated like celebrities here and were comfortable in their element.

That is, until the queen noticed the platform. She actually stopped in her steps. A frown darkened her face as she stared at Adelaide. She said something to Georg and then led the way up the steps to the table. After a brief conversation with the man seated on the far end, the queen and her son took seats next to him. Queen Johanna was clearly unhappy with this seating arrangement.

Albert seemed oblivious to the queen's demeanor as he stood and, after testing the sound system, welcomed everyone to the festivities. Next, he announced the youth choir, which instantly broke into a lively Christmas carol. After two more songs, which the crowd merrily joined into, Albert announced the next entertainment, a charming ballet troupe featuring little girls in fluffy, white tutus trimmed with red velvet. They were followed by a string quartet of white-haired musicians playing "Silent Night."

A short silence followed the old hymn. Then a loud drumroll sounded, and a strange creature—a cross between Bigfoot and a devil—ran through the crowd. Children screamed, some with delight and some in genuine fear. The adults looked mostly amused or feigned frightened expressions.

"What is *that*?" Adelaide whispered to Albert.

He laughed. "Krampus."

"Krampus?"

The costumed creature continued running about dramatically, frightening the small children and making the grown-ups laugh before a kindly-looking bearded character dressed in a long white gown and a red satin tunic and headpiece showed up and majestically shook his scepter's gold sphere. Adelaide realized this was Saint Nicholas. His actions seemed to drive Krampus from the square. Everyone cheered, and the children looked relieved.

Another jolly carol was sung and then Albert stood and apologized for the king's absence before asking for the people's prayers for his ill health. Right then and there, everyone quietly bowed their heads, Adelaide assumed, to pray for their king. She was so touched, her eyes got a little teary.

Now, speaking in English, Albert asked Adelaide to stand beside him. "We want to welcome King Max's only daughter." The crowd fell silent, watching with open curiosity and rapt interest as Albert continued. "Princess Adelaide Katelyn comes to us from America. Some of our older citizens may remember the engagement of King Max to the beautiful American woman, Susan Smith, many years ago. That woman has since passed, but her daughter, Princess Adelaide, has graced us with her presence. We are honored to have Princess Adelaide light our tree. But first we will invite Father Bamburg to ask the blessing for our upcoming Advent season."

Suddenly all the strings of electric lights went out and, with the square draped in darkness, the crowd murmured with anticipation as the old priest stepped up and said an Advent blessing, while illuminated by a single candle.

After the prayer, Adelaide, also illuminated by a single candle, was led by Albert to the prop Anton had told her about. It represented the royal Christmas tree light switch. "Do I say anything before I pull it?" she whispered to Albert.

"The king usually says 'Frohes Weihnachtsfest,'" he whispered back.

And so she shouted out the Christmas greeting, and the people returned it. Then she pulled the switch, and just like magic, the huge Christmas tree glimmered over the square with multicolored lights. The crowd cheered, and an oompah band began to play jovial Christmas songs as strings of lights and lanterns lit up again. Some people started to sing while others began dancing. Some left in pursuit of food. All in all, it was a very happy crowd, and Adelaide felt honored to participate in such a meaningful way.

"Would the princess care to dance?" Albert asked.

"I don't really know how to do *that* kind of dance," she confessed.

"I can help you with our little polka. Just a hop, skip, and sidestep to the music. If you're having fun, no one will notice what your feet are doing."

"Unless I step on yours," she said as he led her out with the other dancers.

He took her hand. "Let the music carry you."

To her surprise, after a few missteps, the music did lead her. And it was fun. She'd always loved dancing but had never done anything like this folk dance. After the lively number with Albert ended, Anton invited her to dance and, feeling a tiny bit more confident, she hopped and skipped and jumped with him as well.

They enjoyed a couple more folk songs, then Anton suggested they return to their table. "The mulled wine and ginger-bread are being served there," he said quietly. "We don't want to offend anyone."

While they had danced, some of the seating arrangements had changed. Queen Johanna and Prince Georg now occupied the center seats and did not look inclined to move.

"Make room for Princess Adelaide," Albert said loudly.

"We are fine down here," Adelaide called back. She smiled at Anton as he pulled out a chair for her. They both sat down.

"Good move," Anton whispered to her. "Your humility will win over the people."

"It just seemed the right thing to do." She smiled at a group of citizens who were intently watching her. "Unfortunately, I'm afraid I'm not winning over the queen," she said quietly, returning a happy wave to some grinning children. She wasn't used to this much attention but was trying to take it in stride.

"The queen reminds me of that old saying," he whispered. "If looks could kill, you'd be in trouble. But don't mind her."

They continued to smile, praising the mulled wine and gin-gerbread as they sampled and happily returned greetings to well-wishers in the crowd.

Before long, Adelaide was dancing again, eventually getting so warm that even the queen's icy stares didn't chill her. She shed the beautiful but heavy fur coat and danced with Anton and the villagers. She couldn't remember when she'd ever had so much fun.

Eleven

By now everyone in the palace seemed to know Adelaide, but Anton still insisted upon seeing her inside after the tree-lighting festivities. As he told her good night, he reminded her of the other upcoming Christmas activities.

"King Max is determined to ride in tomorrow's parade with you," Anton informed her as they took the elevator up to her floor, "but my uncle is doubtful his physician will approve of him sitting in the open air for that long."

"I guess I see his point, but it's sad the king is missing out on all the fun."

"Hopefully, he'll save enough strength to attend celebrations here in the palace. As you've seen on the schedule, several events are on the roster."

"Montovia really makes a big deal about Christmas."

He studied her. "How do you feel about that?"

"Oh, don't get me wrong, I love it. Childhood Christmases were pretty lackluster and sparse. I remember thinking everyone else had a lot more fun than Mom and me."

"Well, the first week of December is always busy here. It'll quiet down some after Saint Nicholas Day." He paused as the elevator doors opened. "By the way, your father would be proud of you tonight. You were wonderful, Adelaide. A true princess." His smile gave her a happy rush and for a split second, she thought he might kiss her.

"Thanks." She felt her cheeks flush as she exited the elevator.

"I'll be here at ten in the morning." He tipped his head, pushed the elevator button, and as the doors closed, flashed her another big smile. Despite the long evening and all the dancing, her feet felt light as feathers as she headed to her room.

"Excuse me."

Adelaide pivoted in the hall. Queen Johanna emerged from the royal quarters, almost as if she'd been lurking in wait for her.

"Yes?" Adelaide paused, taking a closer look at the queen's regal gown of burgundy moiré satin and her jeweled necklace and earrings. Very queenly.

"We need to talk." The queen motioned to the room behind her.

Adelaide wasn't so sure they did, but curiosity won out and she followed the queen into the royal living room. Although there was an inviting fire in the hearth, the queen didn't invite her to sit. Instead, she pointed at Adelaide.

"Where did you get that coat?"

"From the king."

She scowled. "And the diamonds? Also from the king?"

Adelaide locked eyes with her, nodding. "That's right."

"Gifts from the king?"

Adelaide considered this. Part of her wanted to admit she planned to return the coat and diamonds, but then she reconsidered. "They belonged to my grandmother, my namesake." She stroked the soft fur. "My father had this coat refashioned for me. I've never felt anything so soft."

The queen pursed her lips. "Queen Adelaide's Russian sable. Very valuable. Too precious for a young girl. And the necklace— too valuable to dance in so carelessly. It could have been lost."

"I made sure the latch was secure," Adelaide said. "And Albert kept an eye on the sable for me. I'm sorry it worried you, but my father entrusted me with these things. And I am not a young girl."

The queen narrowed her eyes. "I fear for the king. His mind is going. It makes him thoughtless and reckless. He is not responsible."

"His mind is going? *Where?*" Adelaide challenged. "I've had long, detailed conversations with him, and he is sharp and clear and focused."

"You do not know what goes on here." The queen folded her arms across her front. "You are only a visitor. The sooner you leave us, the better for the king. For his sake, you should go now."

"My father doesn't want me to go." Adelaide held her ground. "Why would you say that?"

"The king is not well. You stay longer and it will hurt him more. I know your plan to return to your country after Christmas. Why prolong this agony for the king? If you love him, you will go now." She waved her hand dismissively. "It's for the best."

"I know my presence makes you uncomfortable," Adelaide said slowly. "I'm sorry about that. But I came here for my father, and I will stay as long as he wants me to." Of course, even as she said this, she wondered, *What if he wants me here indefinitely?* "Now, if you'll excuse me, I'm tired from the long day. Gute nacht."

Adelaide had never wanted to be treated like a celebrity, but after the Christmas parade and her ride in the beautiful gilt-trimmed carriage, pulled by a gorgeous pair of Percheron horses, she felt pretty special. Her favorite part had been waving to the crowd and tossing candies to the kiddies. Hopefully she was a good representative for the king.

Not far behind her in the parade, Queen Johanna and Prince Georg had ridden in the back of a classic Mercedes-Benz convertible. According to Anton, the king always rode unaccompanied in the royal carriage, with family following. Although Queen Johanna had expected the honor of the carriage ride in his absence, the king had insisted it be Princess Adelaide. Of course, Adelaide knew this would drive the wedge between her and the queen only that much deeper.

"It's no wonder she hates me," Adelaide told Anton as he drove her back to the palace after the parade. "If I weren't here, she and Georg would have all the fanfare to themselves."

"True, but what about the people? They seem to really enjoy your presence. And it pleases the king."

"I know, but I'm still concerned." She shared the queen's warning from last night—how Adelaide's lingering presence might make it harder for the king.

Anton frowned. "Naturally, the queen wants you gone. Any reason is a good reason in her mind. But you can't let her frighten you away."

"She doesn't frighten me. Not really. I mean, I can stand up to her. I just worry that I'm giving my father false hopes that I will remain here . . . well, indefinitely."

Anton's brow furrowed, but he said nothing.

"That was never my plan," she continued. "I tried to make it clear from the start that this is only a visit. Albert encouraged me to come meet my father. I planned to stay through Christmas and then go home and finish my law degree."

"Right." His tone sounded flat.

Adelaide suspected her candid reminder had hurt him. She hadn't meant to be so blunt, but she could see it in his eyes. She had inflicted pain. Whether he felt his friendship rejected or something more, she wasn't sure. But something had changed between them. Something that hurt inside of her as well.

Yet what did he expect from her? What did any of them honestly expect? That she would suddenly give up her homeland and law career to become a Montovian citizen? That she would play the royal princess, ready to inherit her father's throne when the time came? What in life had ever prepared her for such an assignment? Even though she'd been beefing up her knowledge of Montovian law and history, she was a foreigner here.

Neither of them spoke for the last several minutes of the ride, but Anton, as usual, insisted on accompanying her inside the palace. Seeing his glum countenance and knowing she had caused it, she quickly thanked him and said goodbye on the ground floor before she dashed up the stairs—all three flights. Then, filled with confusing and conflicting emotions, she rushed to her room, out of breath, locked the door behind her, and suppressed the urge to cry. And why did she even want to cry? The parade had been delightful. She was a guest in a beautiful palace. Her father was waiting for her report of the parade and to see the photos she'd snapped on her phone. This little misunderstanding with Anton was probably fixable. Why was she so upset?

She slipped out of the sable coat and carefully hung it on the padded hanger before collapsing into the armchair. Not feeling up for much more, she stared blankly out the window where thick dark clouds hung over the rolling hills. Was snow coming?

She closed her eyes and leaned back. She wasn't physically tired but emotionally weary. Was this the challenge of a royal ruler? Torn in different directions, the weight of the country on your shoulders? Hoping to accommodate one person while injuring another? She needed a new adage, like you could please some of the people some of the time . . . Adelaide sighed. Maybe Queen Johanna was right. Maybe she really should go home.

On Sunday, King Max invited Adelaide to attend church with him. Because of his wheelchair, they went early to get situated in the pew reserved for royalty. It was set off to one side of the majestic cathedral. As Adelaide admired the beautiful stained glass windows and listened to the pipe organ, the church began to fill. After a few minutes, the queen and her son were escorted to the royal pew as well. They took their seats on King Max's left. Adelaide smiled stiffly at them, and as usual, Georg returned her smile, but no words were exchanged, and the king kept his gaze fixed forward.

Because it was the official beginning of Advent, it was a special service. Even though it was all in German, Adelaide still felt surprisingly moved by the music, candle lighting, and general ceremony. And she didn't miss the glistening of her father's eyes as he reached for her hand to clasp it warmly in his. Was this his last Christmas?

By the time the service ended, the king was clearly worn out. Seeing this, Queen Johanna immediately took charge. Ordering Herr Schneider and the king's other aide, she seized the role of caring wife and domineering queen, effectively shoving Adelaide aside as she helped King Max to be ushered from the church. The king looked too tired to protest as Adelaide was left in the wake of the queen's melodramatic exit.

Seeing this as her opportunity to walk through the village and do a bit of exploring on her own, Adelaide slipped out of the cathedral almost unnoticed. A few people smiled and waved cheerfully as they recognized her, but dressed in her dark woolen coat, a plain felt hat, and tall boots, she managed to make a smooth getaway.

The village was still quiet, but it was fun to walk freely past the shops, gaze in the windows, and observe all the little details she'd missed before. Like the internet café next to the chocolate shop. Not that she needed to visit there since the palace had its own service, but she'd heard connectivity was patchy within the principality. She paused to look in the toy shop window and admire the Christmas display of merchandise that ranged from old-fashioned handmade wooden playthings to flashier electronic toys.

As she strolled, she noticed lights turning on in some of the shops that were opening up for business. She was just rounding the corner to head up the street that led to the palace when she felt a tap on her shoulder. She turned to see Anton grinning at her.

Relieved to see his happy face, and hoping he'd forgiven her for her abruptness yesterday, she returned his smile. "Hello there."

"May I accompany you?"

She nodded vigorously. "Of course."

"Have you time for coffee?" he asked.

"I'd love a coffee."

"They should be open now." He pointed to the coffee shop across the street.

As they crossed, she told him about how she'd spent eight years working in a coffeehouse.

"Really?" He looked surprised. "I can't imagine you serving coffees up from behind a counter."

"You forget I was working to put myself through law school."

His eyes twinkled as he held the door open for her. "A veritable Cinderella."

"In a way."

He led her to a table by the window, then pulled out her chair like a true gentleman. "Not growing up like royalty has its benefits."

"Oh, trust me, I've seen Georg. I'm glad I wasn't raised like that. I have no regrets."

"I can see that. And I understand your desire to return to

your country and your old way of life." He pursed his lips. "I realize it's not fair for us to expect anything more from you than just an enjoyable visit. My uncle and I discussed this for quite some time last night."

She didn't know what to say, and since the barista was asking for their orders, she distracted herself with ordering a latte and a hazelnut croissant. But after the barista left, Adelaide tried to organize her thoughts. She wanted to explain her position to Anton.

"I'm aware that my father, and perhaps others too, would like me to remain in Montovia. I'm sure it seems only natural that I'd want to stay. Not every young woman is offered a palace, furs, jewels—it's a little girl's dream. But I realize there's much more to this. Being the ruler of a small kingdom is no small task."

"That's true. But, as you know, Montovia is not a sole monarchy."

"Yes, but even in a constitutional monarchy, the ruler plays a large role in leadership. Not to mention their royal veto power over Parliament as well as being the tiebreaker vote for issues where Parliament is divided."

"You *have* been doing your homework." His brows arched.

"That's a big responsibility. Especially for a newcomer to the royal family and to Montovia."

"Yet a newcomer with a certain educational background, intelligence, and sensibility could prove a great asset to the principality." His smile was enticing.

She smiled back at him as their order was set on the table.

"Listen, Adelaide," he spoke with intensity after the barista left, "I understand your reluctance, but I'd like you to understand our urgency. Why we hope you'll at least consider our position."

She nodded. "I'm listening."

Now he described how Montovia was often split between the haves and have-nots. "As you know, I grew up in the Gruber province. Mining is the main industry, and although everyone in our province works very hard, when it comes to funding for things like schools, roads, public safety, and such, we are always scrabbling. The wealthier provinces can often be split on issues that affect us, but King Max has always been sympathetic to our causes. Because of his generous vote, we will get a new secondary school next year, and we hope to begin on a much-needed new fire station following that."

"That sounds encouraging." She sipped her latte.

"Yes, it does—right now. But if King Max is replaced by Georg, with the queen mother in his ear, we might lose those very necessary improvements."

"Oh." Adelaide nodded. She could easily imagine the queen taking a hard-nosed position like that. "So having a fair and compassionate ruler is important."

"Vitally important."

"But why me? What happened to my uncle? Do you think Prince Farcus has hidden because he's worried about his throne responsibilities? What were his leanings?"

"Farcus is a good man. Perhaps not as well-suited to leadership as King Max, but we believed he would grow into it. And we believed he was ready to accept the crown."

"Then where is he?" She set her coffee cup down with a clunk. "Why can't he be located?"

"Believe me, we are working on it. All we now know is he actually did leave Scotland at the end of his fishing trip. Not on the flight he'd originally booked, but we were able to trace a ticket in his name from a few days later. But it's been about six weeks now."

"That's a long time to be missing. Where was his flight headed?"

"Vienna. And we know he arrived there. That was about six weeks ago. After that, we assumed he had planned to travel home by train since he's always enjoyed that, but that's where the trail ends."

"Have his cell phone and credit cards been traced?"

"Yes, of course. But nothing."

Adelaide glanced at the young couple at a nearby table, their heads bent together in a romantic gesture, then she looked back at Anton. "Well, it seems mysterious that he would disappear in Vienna."

"We have investigators there trying to figure it out. But still nothing. One investigator clings to the theory that Farcus never actually flew from Edinburgh to Vienna."

"How is that?"

"The theory is Farcus hired someone to fly in his place, then he went in a different direction in a search for anonymity. But my uncle and I don't believe that."

"Because you think he really did want to rule Montovia."

"I think he did." Anton looked down at his coffee. "My worry is that he is dead."

"From foul play?"

He shrugged. "Possibly. It wouldn't be the first time an heir to a throne was, uh, disposed of." He paused to look at her. "And I suppose if that was what happened to your uncle, well, I wouldn't feel very good about encouraging you to step into a position of leadership."

"But what about Montovia?" She suddenly felt a sense of responsibility for her father's homeland.

He shrugged again. "I guess we'd have to make the best of things with Georg."

"And Johanna." She felt a twinge of guilt. Would that mean saying goodbye to Gruber's school and the fire station and who knew what else? It really did not seem fair.

Twelve

O n Monday, Adelaide's afternoon visit with the king was cut short by his physician, who had come at the queen's request. "We will make up for it tomorrow afternoon," her father called to her as the nurse ushered her out.

Seeing the gloomy weather outside, Adelaide returned to her room with the two books her father had just given her. But as she closed her door, she felt torn. The more time she spent with the king, the more she felt pulled into his world. The love of his country was so strong within him that it seemed to seep over onto her. Was it possible she could learn to love this foreign country like he did? Maybe it wasn't as "foreign" as she'd assumed. But for her to rule Montovia—would anyone take her seriously?

She set the books on the table by her chair with a long sigh. Even if she were doing this only to please her father, she knew she had to give it her best effort. She opened the volume on recent Montovian history. Of course, it was written in German. Although she was becoming more fluent, it was still a challenge. So, with her language translation app handy, she proceeded to read up on Montovia's post–World War II history. It was actually fairly mundane, which was probably good. And there was not one word mentioned about King Max's brief affair with the beautiful American woman in the 1990s.

After a while, she picked up the book on Montovian traditions, celebrations, and holidays, going to the section her father had suggested she read after she'd inquired about Krampus Day, which was tomorrow.

Krampus, it seemed, was a bad-natured character. He was described as a half-goat, half-demon monster that terrorized children at Christmastime. *Lovely*, she thought. She'd already witnessed the devilish costumed figure in action the other night, but she still couldn't comprehend how parents allowed their children to be terrorized by such a fiendish creature. As the story went, Krampus was part of the pagan winter solstice rituals. He was the son of Hel and the underworld. When Christians transformed solstice celebrations into Christmas traditions, Saint Nicholas became the grandfatherly figure who rewarded good children with treats and presents on the sixth of December, but Krampus remained on hand as a threat to punish naughty children by leaving them sticks instead of treats.

Some people held Krampus parties on the eve of Saint Nicholas Day. From the king's description, they sounded more like Halloween parties than Christmas ones. "I've never been overly fond of them," he'd told her before she'd been shooed away. "Too much alcohol and ghastly devilish costumes. More for adults than children."

She wanted to ask why she had heard the palace was hosting a Krampus party tomorrow night if he didn't approve, but she'd never gotten the chance. Perhaps she'd get to ask tomorrow. By the time she finished reading, it was dark outside, and although it was the dinner hour, she had no intention of dining with Georg and the queen. Thanks to Anton, she'd acquired a small fridge and was in the habit of stocking it with food items to supplement her "skipped" meals. Naturally, she always sent a politely written excuse. She felt certain the queen appreciated her absences almost as much as Adelaide did.

After a restless night's sleep troubled by dreams about Krampus monsters chasing her around the palace, Adelaide got up early. Her meeting with the king wasn't scheduled until that afternoon, but hungry for a real breakfast and wanting some fresh air, she sent a text to Anton, asking for a recommendation of a breakfast place in the village. Or maybe she was sending him a hint. As a result, he offered to meet her at the palace and introduce her to a little restaurant named Otto's.

As they walked, she asked about the palace's Krampus party. "Am I expected to attend?"

"Expected?" He thought about this for a second before answering. "Well, as a member of the royal family, you probably are expected. But that doesn't mean you have to go."

"My father isn't going."

"No, I would think not."

"Who *does* attend this kind of party?"

"Some dignitaries, people of influence. The queen makes the guest list."

Adelaide nodded. "Right. And they wear costumes?"

"Of a sort. Some wear furry headdresses with horns. Some go all out with devil costumes, forks and tails, you know. Most just don extravagant or provocative evening wear."

"Do you go?"

"I've gone in the past. But it's not really my cup of tea."

"Do you think I should go?" she asked.

He rubbed his chin as they waited at the intersection for a bus to pass by. "Well, that depends. If you plan to stay on here, I guess it could be, uh, educational. Otherwise, I'd suggest you steer clear of it."

"If I did decide to go, would you consider being my escort?" She felt a rush of nerves as she braced herself for his answer.

"Sure." He brightened and, taking her arm, scooted them

across the street before the next vehicle came. Soon they were seated by a fireplace in what looked like an old-fashioned German pub. As they dined on eggs and sausages, she asked what he would suggest she wear for the party.

"I don't want to wear a costume," she told him, "but I don't want to stick out like a sore thumb either."

"Like a *sore thumb*?" He laughed. "What's that supposed to mean?"

"I guess it's American slang." She shrugged. "But I wonder what I could wear to help me to fit in. Nothing scandalous, of course, but—"

"Sounds like you need to visit Stilvoll again."

"The women's dress shop?"

"Yes." He checked his watch. "Most shops open at nine during Christmas season. I'll venture Stilvoll will open soon."

After breakfast, Anton walked her down to the dress shop where, once again, Frieda helped Adelaide pick out a dress that was appropriate for her royal event. The ruby red satin gown with its slightly plunging neckline wasn't something she would've worn normally, but for tonight's party, Frieda assured Adelaide, it would be considered conservative. Agreeing to a slight alteration, Frieda promised to have it delivered to the palace by five, and Adelaide, with Anton carrying the bag that contained a pair of pretty red shoes, made it back to the palace before noon.

"Thank you." She took the bag from him. "I guess I'll see you tonight at seven?"

"I'm actually looking forward to it now." He tipped his head. "See you then."

After Adelaide put her shoes away, she sat down to read a bit more from the history book. Her appointment with her father wasn't until two, but by one thirty, she felt hungry. Thinking she'd fix them a small tea tray, Adelaide let herself into the royal family kitchen. The king had assured her that she could use it as needed, but she still felt a bit like an interloper as she heated a kettle and laid a few snacks out on a serving tray. Fortunately, the royal quarters, as usual, were not occupied. By now, Adelaide knew the queen had a schedule that kept her away quite a bit during the day. What she did was a mystery, but it did make it easier for Adelaide to come and go.

The kettle had just boiled when Adelaide heard a cell phone ringing from the dining room. Thinking it was probably Georg, possibly looking for her, Adelaide turned off the flame and tried to be silent so he wouldn't notice her and would soon go. But a woman's voice answered with a brusque "Hallo?" Then, speaking in German, the woman's tone became vexed. Adelaide recognized the queen's voice and could translate some of the words. Not enough to make complete sense, but enough to feel serious concern. What was going on?

Using the notepad on her own phone, Adelaide made skeletal notes of the conversation, including some phonetic spellings of German words she didn't know and names that seemed of interest. She heard the queen's abrupt "adieu" and the sound of heels echoing through the dining room followed by the firm shut of the door. Adelaide let out a deep breath. Something about that conversation felt very suspicious and, although she was tempted to discuss it with the king, she worried that it might prove stressful for him.

She shot a text message to Anton, explaining she hadn't meant to eavesdrop but had been trapped in the kitchen and now felt certain that something was amiss with the queen. She told him how she'd made notes about the conversation, and he asked her to send them. After she did so, she noticed the time and hurried to get the tea tray ready. Sending one last text, she told Anton she needed to meet with her father but hoped they could talk afterward. He promised to be at the palace waiting for her.

With an expression of nonchalance on her face, in case the

queen was still about, Adelaide carried the tray through the living room and directly into the king's private quarters, where she was greeted by Herr Schneider.

"The king is eager to see you," he said quietly, "but your visit must be short. The physician comes again at three."

She tightened her grip on the tea tray. "Is anything wrong?"

"Nothing to concern you." His expression was impossible to read, but for some reason, she questioned his words. Something seemed to be troubling him. Still, she kept her doubts to herself and smiled brightly as she carried the tray to the king, then waited as Herr Schneider set up a table for the two of them.

Hoping the king didn't suspect anything out of the ordinary, she talked about the history she'd read and informed him she planned to attend the Krampus party tonight. "It's not so much that I want to go, but Anton suggested I should . . . just to see and understand what it's all about."

King Max nodded. "That is wise. This party is not a tradition I enjoy, but I have allowed the queen to do as she liked with it these last few years. She felt the celebration was important. I am not so sure. I will be very interested in your opinion." He frowned slightly. "But do be careful, mein lieber. Sometimes I believe unscrupulous people take advantage of the merriments."

"Anton will be my escort."

He smiled. "You are in good hands then."

They visited until the physician arrived again. After apologizing to Adelaide, he explained the need for new blood tests.

"And I thought bloodletting went out in the 1800s," the king teased.

Adelaide laughed, promising to give her father the full report of tonight's party tomorrow. He reminded her again to be careful.

She'd barely left the king's quarters when Anton met her in the hall. "Albert is downstairs. He wants you to tell us everything you overheard earlier." His words were hushed, and he glanced over his shoulder as he said them. "I'll take you to him."

In one of the Parliament offices, the three of them sat down behind closed doors. Anton made notes on a legal pad as Albert questioned Adelaide regarding the queen's phone conversation. With her phone's notes pulled up, Adelaide tried to replay all that she could recall.

"You think she was speaking to a man named Steffen, and you heard her mention Farcus?"

"It was Farcus's name that got my attention," she explained. "I know King Max's brother's name is Farcus, so when the queen said 'losschlagen Farcus' several times in a very urgent way, I started listening closely. It felt as if she were arguing with this Steffen person, or perhaps just trying to persuade him. I haven't had a chance to look to see what *losschlagen* means."

Albert crossed his arms in front of him. "It means do away with."

"She wants to do away with Farcus?" Adelaide felt her own eyes grow wide. "As in kill him?"

He frowned. "It does sound very extreme, but it's not impossible."

"Who is Steffen?" she asked.

"The queen has a brother-in-law named Steffen," Anton explained. "He is her deceased husband's brother. She's always been quite close to him."

Albert pointed to Adelaide. "You also said she mentioned your name."

"Yes," Adelaide checked the notes on her phone. "She used another word I'm not familiar with, but I tried to write it down phonetically." She attempted to pronounce it.

"Beseitigen?" Anton repeated.

"Yes. That sounds right," she confirmed. "What does it mean?"

"It's similar to losschlagen. It means eliminate. To remove something."

"Like me?"

"You're certain she said these things?" Albert asked, his eyes locked on hers. "That you heard her right, Adelaide? Are you sure?"

"Yes. I heard her use Farcus's name several times in that vexed sort of urgent tone. My name only came up at the end of the conversation." Adelaide didn't admit that the way the queen said her name sounded like she'd tasted poison. "She didn't sound quite so urgent, but she was intense."

"She wants to ensure the crown for Prince Georg," Anton told Albert. "That has to be the motivation."

Albert nodded, his eyes downcast. "So it seems."

"So she's gotten Farcus out of her way. And Steffen is involved somehow."

"The good news is that Farcus must still be alive, but it sounds like the queen wants him gone permanently." Albert faced Adelaide, his brow creased. "And perhaps you as well."

She simply nodded, trying to absorb what felt like a weird old movie plot as Anton grasped her hand and turned to his uncle. "Is Adelaide safe in the palace?"

"Possibly not." Albert was already dialing something on his phone.

Adelaide blinked. "Really? Do you honestly think the queen would go to such extremes? What if she were found out?"

"Queen Johanna is a very driven woman. We've suspected for some time she is romantically involved with Steffen," Albert said. "And like Farcus, Steffen has been missing for a couple of months now."

"Which no longer seems coincidental." Anton's brow furrowed with concern.

"What about Prince Farcus? Will he be safe?" Adelaide's stomach was tying into knots.

"We need to take Queen Johanna in for questioning," Albert said solemnly.

"And examine her cell phone records," Anton added.

"What about Georg?" Albert turned to Adelaide. "Did you hear his name mentioned in that conversation?"

She shook her head.

"I will call the chief of police right now," Albert told Anton as he stood. "You stay here with Adelaide. Don't let her out of your sight."

Anton nodded, still holding on to Adelaide's hand. She offered him a grateful smile, but everything about this felt so surreal. At the other end of the room, Albert talked into his phone.

"We must be very clandestine," Albert said, instructing someone to send the police chief to the palace immediately. "Send a couple of plainclothes officers with him. And no sirens." He told them where to meet, then hung up. "You two stay in here with the door locked. Don't talk to anyone. I will attempt to locate the queen and her son without tipping them off. Then I'll talk to the chief."

Albert left and Anton locked the door behind him. He crossed the room, then sat down across the table from her with a perplexed expression.

"What if I'm wrong about this?" Adelaide asked quietly. "What if I misheard her?"

"I suppose it would be embarrassing . . . but also a relief."

"Do you really think the queen is capable of something so diabolical?"

"Not personally. But she could hire someone." He shook his head. "With power-hungry people, anything is possible. And we know she likes money. King Max used to keep her spending under control, but since he became ill, the budget seems to have gone by the wayside."

"What if they can't find her?"

"That crossed my mind too, but the police chief should know

what to do." Anton squeezed her hand again. "Try not to worry. What will be will be."

How could she not worry? If the queen wanted to knock off Farcus and possibly Adelaide too, it seemed unlikely she could commit these crimes without assistance. But who would she be working with? Adelaide doubted it would be Georg. But she understood why Albert had told them to stay put and speak to no one. Other than Anton, Albert, and her father, Adelaide wasn't sure who could be trusted in the kingdom. It seemed a great deal of risk and trouble in order to gain power over such a tiny principality. But, not for the first time, Adelaide felt she was in over her head. With Anton still holding her hand, she closed her eyes and silently asked God for help and for protection—for all of them.

Thirteen

Not surprisingly, the queen was not in the palace. And Georg, according to Albert, seemed completely and believably oblivious. "This is the plan the chief is hatching," Albert told Anton and Adelaide later in the afternoon. "We want you to attend tonight's party as planned. We will all be there. Some in costume. We will all do surveillance. If anyone sees anything suspicious, they are to text this number." He set down a card, allowing Anton and Adelaide to copy the number into their phones. "Then everyone on surveillance will be notified."

"So the queen will just freely move about the party?" Anton asked.

"Yes. The chief hopes she will connect with her cohorts. He already has phone records that point to certain players. He is optimistic we will wrap this all up in short order."

"Really?" Adelaide asked. "Is there a chance Farcus will be found?"

"Our investigators are on it. They traced the queen's last phone call to the Vienna area," Albert explained. "They suspect Farcus may be at the family villa."

"But wouldn't he have called?" Adelaide asked.

"Not if he's being held against his will." Albert pocketed the business card. "And our investigators have checked the villa numerous times. It's closed for the season. Quiet as a tomb."

"Hopefully not Farcus's tomb," Anton said quietly.

She cringed at the thought. "Poor man. I hope and pray he's still alive."

"Does the king know about any of this?" Anton asked.

"Not yet." Albert frowned. "We don't want to worry him until we know more."

"Yes, of course."

Albert pointed to Adelaide. "Anton will go with you to your room. Pack an overnight bag with the things you'll need for tonight's festivities. You are not safe at the palace for now."

"What about the king?" she asked. "Is he safe?"

Albert pursed his lips. "We see no reason the queen would want him gone. Not just yet."

Adelaide nodded. "That makes sense. But do you really think she's that worried that I could replace him?"

"Yes." Anton opened the door for her, and they waved good-bye to Albert. "That's why we must keep an eye on you."

Although assured the queen was not in residence at the moment, Adelaide still felt like looking over her shoulder as she and Anton went to her room. He waited outside her opened door while she quickly packed everything she needed, then she remembered that her gown wouldn't be delivered until five. She asked Anton where to have it sent.

"We'll pick it up on our way," he said quietly. "We don't want to disclose where you'll be staying."

"This is kind of exciting," she said as he drove her through the village a little while later. They'd picked up her party dress and then stopped by his apartment where he got his own things. "I feel like we're in a spy movie. My mother loved James Bond. I was never much of a fan, but now I wish I'd watched more."

Anton laughed. "Not sure how much that would help you now. Mostly you need to remember to be careful tonight. Please don't get out of my sight."

"So, where are you taking us now?"

"To my good friend Gerard's home. Rather, Gerard's parents' home. It's not far from the village, but it's in the country. Not fancy but very private." He explained how Gerard's father was a farmer and a hunter. "He has quite an impressive gun collection."

"Guns?" She felt alarmed. "Do you think that's necessary?"

"No, but it makes me feel more protected somehow."

The Baumann farm was enchanting. Dozens of woolly sheep comfortably grazed in fenced green pastures, and colorful chickens were roaming around closer to the house. The barn was an architectural treasure of stone and wood timbers. And the farmhouse, with its white stucco walls, thick thatched roof, and windows glowing with golden light, was like a page from a picture book.

The Baumanns' were expecting them upon their arrival. They welcomed Anton with hugs and greeted Adelaide like a long-lost relative. Delicious smells wafted in from the kitchen. Adelaide had never felt so at home. Like Anton had said, the Baumanns' house wasn't fancy, but it was warm and cozy. All thoughts of the ice queen and chilly palace were put aside as the four of them sat at a rough wooden table to eat generous bowls of the tastiest stew Adelaide had ever tasted. And for dessert, they ate apple strudel topped with thick cream.

"I heard they are serving food at the palace party tonight," Adelaide said to Frau Baumann while Herr Baumann showed Anton his newest hunting rifle. "But I won't touch a bit of it after this."

"Ach, palace food is not good for digestion," Frau Baumann said with her thick German accent. "Now I take you to room." She led her up the stairs to a small dormer-style room. "My

117

daughter. Her room." She smiled as she patted the faded patch-work quilt on the bed. "My mutter, she make this."

Practicing her German, Adelaide complimented her on the quilt and the room, then asked the age of her daughter, which got Frau Baumann talking quickly. She said her daughter was forty and her son was thirty-five. Before Adelaide could re-spond, she was listing off the names and ages of her grand-children and where they all lived and worked, most of which went over Adelaide's head.

"Now you rest . . . refresh." Frau Baumann patted her solidly on the back. "You have big nacht ahead, jawohl?"

Adelaide nodded. "Ja."

Dressed in her red satin gown, the diamond necklace, and the Russian sable coat, Adelaide knew she should feel like a million bucks as they entered the palace. Instead, she felt like a bundle of raw nerves. By now they knew, via text messages from a police detective, the queen had been playing host with Georg by her side. Anton, who looked dashingly handsome in a black tux with a red vest, said it was a strategic political move on the queen's part. Showing the VIPs in attendance that she was still in charge and Georg was still prepared for the throne, the queen wanted to get and maintain the upper hand.

And when Adelaide spotted the queen, dressed in a very low-cut, formfitting gown with daring slits up one side of her skirt, her jaw dropped. Queen Johanna looked very unqueenly, and Adelaide doubted King Max would approve. Still, the queen smiled and greeted her guests like she owned not just the palace but the whole world as well. Meanwhile Georg was nowhere in sight.

When the queen noticed Adelaide and Anton join the recep-tion line, her perfect red-lipped smile faltered ever so slightly, and her pale blue eyes looked icier than ever. Even so, she grasped Adelaide's hands and greeted her. "I did not expect you tonight," she said. "Georg said you left. We thought to America."

"No, not yet. My father suggested I might enjoy tonight's festivities. Thank you for inviting me." Adelaide freed her hands from the queen's chilly ones and stepped aside.

"Watch out for Krampus tonight." The queen's tone was light, but her expression was not. "He's out to get the bad little boys and girls."

"Then Adelaide should have no worries," Anton told the queen.

The queen laughed like this was amusing, but Adelaide suspected she would love nothing more than to turn Krampus loose on her inconvenient stepdaughter.

Anton, with his arm nestled around hers, led Adelaide toward the ballroom, where a hard rock song was being played by a loud band dressed like devils. Already a number of couples were on the dance floor, letting loose with some wild moves that made Adelaide blush. The alcohol must've been flowing freely for a while.

"Can I get you a drink?" Anton asked.

"Only if it's a soft drink."

"Exactly what I had in mind, but I will make sure it looks like something stronger." He winked. "Help us to fit in here better."

"Brilliant." She smiled.

"Don't move from this spot," he warned, and she agreed. She watched as he went over to the bar, which was crowded with a rowdy bunch. Then she turned her attention to people watching partiers of all ages. The majority appeared older than her and Anton. Dressed in a variety of costumes, they mingled and danced and drank, acting, she thought, like a bunch of inebriated adolescents.

"There's my favorite princess." Georg sidled up to her suddenly. "I thought you were gone."

"Gone?"

"I saw you leave with Anton. You had your bags with you. I thought you went home." He held up his amber-filled glass with a slightly foggy expression.

"Did you *hope* I went home?" she asked a bit coyly, hoping to extract some information.

"No, no, I like you, Adelaide. I like you a lot." He leaned closer, his breath heavy with whatever drink was in his glass.

"I like you too, Georg. But I'm afraid your mother does not like me."

His shoulders sank. "Ja, that is true."

"Why does she hate me so much?" Adelaide asked innocently. "I have done nothing to her."

"Ha! Nothing, you say?" He leaned toward her, pointing to her diamond necklace. "That is not nothing, mein lieber."

She didn't like him using her father's term of endearment but continued to smile just the same. "But don't you think a princess should wear fine jewelry?"

"Ja, I do. If you were my princess, I would give you bigger, better jewels."

"I believe you would." She tilted her head to one side, playing the coquette. "But tell me something, Georg, and please be honest with me. Do you really, truly want to be king?"

His brow furrowed as he pressed his lips into a tight line, as if thinking hard. And then he smiled again. "If you were queen, Adelaide, I would want to be king."

"But your mother wants to be queen, Georg. She would never let me be your queen." She tapped him on his chest. "You would have to be king without me. But you would have your mother acting as your queen."

He puffed out his chest. "I wouldn't let her be queen."

"She might not wear the crown, but she would be ruling. And what about our uncle? Prince Farcus may be coming back." She studied him closely, but his expression looked sincerely surprised.

"Coming back here? To Montovia?"

"Yes. That's what I heard."

"My mother said Farcus was gone for good."

"How would she know that?"

He shrugged. "She just knows. That's all. Now, Adelaide, please say you'll be my queen."

"I can't be your queen. Your mother won't allow it. You know that, Georg. Even though you're a grown man, she rules over you. She tells you what to do."

"No." He frowned deeply, then downed the remainder of his drink. "If I am king, my mother cannot tell me what to do."

"Oh, but she will." Adelaide was sincere with him now. "You know she wants to rule Montovia through you. You would be king in name only. Just a figurehead. Your mother would rule the principality. You must know that by now."

He grabbed one of her hands. "That is why I need you, Adelaide. If you were queen, my mother could *not* rule."

She slowly nodded. "That is true, but that's not what your mother wants." She spotted Anton returning with their drinks. "Would you ever be able to stand up against your mother, Georg?"

He just stared at her, but the answer was written in his eyes.

"Here's your drink." Anton handed her something pink with a cherry in it.

She took a cautious sniff. "Thank you."

"How are you, Georg?" Anton asked with genuine interest.

"Mad as Krampus." He glared at Anton.

Anton leaned back a bit. "At me?"

"No. Just mad is all. I need another drink." Georg turned back to Adelaide. "I meant what I said."

She just nodded. "I know you did. Take care now, Georg."

As the prince stomped off, Anton asked what he had been talking about.

"Oh, just that he wants to make me his queen." She sipped

her overly sweet soda. "But I learned something else. I don't think he knows anything about his mother's involvement in whatever is going on with Prince Farcus. I'm pretty good at reading people, and Georg is in the dark. Well, except for knowing his mother wants to control him as queen. I think he gets that."

"Poor Georg." Anton shook his head.

"Poor Montovia if he ever gets to be king."

The band started to play a slower number, and Anton asked her to dance. "That way we can keep an eye on the crowd," he said.

"Yes, of course." As she danced with him, Adelaide temporarily forgot about their surveillance assignment. She lost herself in Anton's arms and wished this moment could last forever.

But the song ended and after a brief pause, the drummer began to pound furiously on his instrument to get everyone's attention. Suddenly the lights dimmed, and a spotlight shone brightly onto a hairy beast with horns, hooves, and creepy fangs. This evil-looking Krampus dramatically entered the ballroom to the beat of the drum, letting out a bloodcurdling shriek as he prowled among the guests. Adelaide cringed and moved closer to Anton.

But others cheered as the Krampus pretended to terrorize. Growling and stalking, the monster worked the crowd, pointing out the "bad children," which amused many. He paused near Adelaide and Anton as the houselights went off. Aside from a few flickering candles on the sidelines, the ballroom was eerily black. Adelaide felt the growling Krampus drawing closer—and then she was snatched from Anton's grasp and dragged away screaming while everyone else just laughed.

CHAPTER

Fourteen

The hem of Adelaide's dress got torn in the scuffle that followed her bizarre abduction, but other than being shaken, she was okay. The man dressed as Krampus claimed it was all just a joke, but Anton and the two plainclothes officers who'd tackled him out in the main hall were not amused. And as Adelaide listened to the chief grill her abductor, she, too, began to see the seriousness of what she'd assumed was a random albeit startling incident.

Huddled with them in a small office off the main hall, the Krampus, a.k.a. Hugo Scholer, had removed his headpiece to expose messy blond hair and a flushed youthful face. Pressure from the chief soon convinced Hugo to admit he'd been paid to snatch the "pretty American frau in the red dress." But Hugo still claimed it was only for laughs.

When the police chief asked if he realized he'd just abducted King Max's daughter, the *Princess* Adelaide, Hugo's blue eyes grew wide with fear. "Nein, nein." He held up his hands, now freed from the hairy gloves and sharp claws, and eagerly surrendered the name of the man who'd hired him for this "little joke."

The police chief then demanded to know where Hugo had

been instructed to take the princess, and he sheepishly confessed he was to take her "downstairs to the ground floor to where friends would transport her to the dungeon to lock her up. But only as a joke, of course."

The chief exchanged glances with his team, instructing two of them to hurry down there and discreetly take Hugo's cohorts into custody. Next, he told his lieutenant to transport Hugo over to the station for a full statement and booking. Although Adelaide felt a little sorry for the young man, who now looked close to tears, she hoped it would be a good life lesson. After all, she might've had a weak heart and expired down in the dark, dreary dungeon.

When they were gone, the chief turned to Adelaide. "I cannot let you return to the party."

She shrugged. "Fine by me, but why?"

"Too dangerous. But another reason—those involved in the scheme must not know it failed. Not yet."

Adelaide was pretty sure she understood. "That way you can keep watching them."

"Exactly." He turned to Anton. "Take Adelaide back to the farmhouse. Keep her there until I advise you otherwise. Und you must not be observed leaving the palace." He pointed to a box filled with random items. "Left from our costumes. You can disguise yourselves."

Adelaide lifted up a purple hooded cape trimmed with mangy fur and suddenly remembered her father's gift. "What about my Russian sable coat?"

"That's right, I checked it for her," Anton told the chief.

"I will take care of it." He placed a hand on Anton's shoulder. "Get her out of here. Quickly und quietly."

The chief left and Anton and Adelaide outfitted themselves in strange ensembles. They made their exit through the quiet main hall. "I don't think anyone noticed us," Adelaide whispered as they hurried out to his Land Rover.

"We'll take a circuitous route just in case." He started the engine. Before long, they were cruising through the countryside without a single car in sight.

"So, that was supposed to be a Christmas celebration?" Adelaide just shook her head. "No wonder the king doesn't approve."

"It's not my cup of tea, that's for sure. And when that Krampus grabbed you like that." He blew out a long breath. "I almost wished for Herr Baumann's new hunting rifle, I was that angry."

She couldn't help but smile at the image of Anton, dressed in a tuxedo, aiming a hunting rifle at the crazy Krampus. "Poor Hugo. I think he was in over his head."

"Hopefully the police will knock some sense into him."

"I know the police chief wants me to stay at the farmhouse until he thinks it's safe, but what about my father? He expected me to visit with him tomorrow."

"We can schedule a phone call. Maybe you can do Facetime or Zoom."

"Does the king know how to do that?" she asked.

"He has people to help him."

"Yes, of course." She nodded. "I just don't want him to worry about me." But it was more than that. It was hard to process completely, but she was feeling more drawn into her father's quirky little kingdom. She cared more about its future and its citizens than she had anticipated. And if she were being completely honest, she cared about Anton too.

The Baumanns were happy to have Adelaide and Anton over for Saint Nicholas Day. With children and grandchildren coming for a late lunch and celebration, there was much to be done, and Adelaide was happy to help out. In the morning, Frau Baumann put her to work making Vanillekipferl, which were crescent-shaped cookies with lots of vanilla and powdered sugar. They practically melted in her mouth.

"Saint Nicholas Day began last night for kinder," Frau Baumann told her. "But we stretch it out with our own traditions." Frau Baumann stirred in the ingredients for the mulled wine that would simmer on the stove. "We like our family to be here. With us. For a happy daytime party. Not like your Krampus party last night." She frowned with disapproval, most likely remembering what little they'd shared about last night's fiasco. "What happened at the palace. Not good."

"No, it was not good. I'm so grateful you don't mind us staying with you awhile longer. Thank you for your hospitality."

"Oh, you are very welcome. We not always have royalty here. But when we do, we like it." Her smile widened as she sampled the mulled wine.

Adelaide gazed out the window toward the nearby hillside where Herr Baumann had taken Anton hunting earlier that morning. She'd never had any experience with hunters, but seeing the two men loaded up with rifles and all, well, she just hoped they'd be safe. "The sky is so dark and gray," she said to her hostess.

"Ja, ja. They say snow coming."

"Will that trouble the hunters?"

"Oh, nein. Snow is good for hunting. Quiet . . . and good tracks to follow."

"Right. It must be beautiful out here when it snows."

"Oh, ja, it is. White and clean. I love first snow."

After finishing in the kitchen, Adelaide helped Frau Baumann wrap up little treats and prizes for the children. It was their tradition to hide them around the house, as well as to tie some onto the Christmas tree.

"We tell the kinder, Saint Nicholas, he come here too. Not only their house." She chuckled. "Und not that horrid old Krampus. We do not let him in."

"Your Saint Nicholas is like our Santa Claus." Adelaide straightened the bow on one of the gifts. "Only Santa Claus makes his arrival on Christmas Eve, when children are sleeping. But the tradition is similar. Children are taught to be good so Santa will bring them something."

"Ja. Good things for good kinder. Und we have only *good* kinder in our family." She laughed heartily. "So we say."

At eleven o'clock, the Baumanns' phone rang. Anton and Albert had prearranged a call from the king, and Adelaide had a nice long conversation with her father. She felt somewhat relieved that he'd been filled in on some of last night's activities. She didn't like the idea of the king being completely in the dark. But at the same time, she didn't want to say too much.

"Albert assures me that this business will soon be wrapped up," he finally said in a weary tone. "And you will come back to the palace. The police chief says by the end of the week."

She wanted to inquire about Queen Johanna and Prince Georg, probably more out of curiosity than concern. She really wanted to ask about Prince Farcus, but unsure of how much the king knew about his brother, she kept quiet to avoid troubling him.

"I hope he's right about the weekend," she said. "But don't worry about me. I am staying in a lovely farmhouse." She told him about what they'd been baking and doing that morning. "I'm having a delightful time, but I do miss you."

"I miss you too, mein lieber."

"Yes. And you are always in my prayers, Father."

"And you in mine. Please, do not worry. God will work out his plans in his time."

She liked that. "God's plan in God's time," she echoed. "I'll hang on to that thought. Thank you."

There was a long pause and then he spoke in a slightly choked voice. "I love you, mein leiber. Whatever happens, I need you to know that. I love you. Your visit has brought me more happiness than I ever believed possible. I am sorry for the years we missed, but God was good to bring you to me when he did."

She felt a lump in her throat. "I love you too, Father. Being with you has made me incredibly happy too. I never imagined what it would feel like to have a father. Thank you for being such a good one."

"If I am good, God be praised." He coughed. "And God be with you, mein leiber. Always."

"God be with you too. Always." She heard a hoarse whisper of adieu, and the click of the phone being hung up. Blinking back tears, she replaced the receiver on the farm's old-fashioned phone and excused herself to her room.

The spicy, sweet aroma of mulled wine wafted up the stairs as the Baumanns' family members began to fill the house with their laughter and merriment down below. Adelaide knew it was time to set aside her concerns for her father and join the party below. After being introduced to everyone, she took a seat by the fire and watched as the grandchildren began their hunt for the Saint Nicholas treats.

"The hunters are not back yet," Frau Baumann quietly told Adelaide.

She frowned. "Is that a problem?"

"Nein, it is good." She laughed as her grandchildren scrambled about, squealing joyfully as they discovered treats tucked into the tree, as well as other clever places, like their grandpa's slippers or grandma's garden boots. Everything about this felt like such a bright contrast to last night's weird Krampus party. Outside, fat snowflakes were starting to tumble down, filling the children with even more excitement. All of it felt like good medicine to Adelaide. Just what she needed to get back into a holiday spirit.

Shortly before noon, the hunters did come home. While shaking snow off their jackets and removing their boots, Herr Baumann announced that their hunt had been successful. There would be venison roast for Christmas.

Soon they were all crowded around the long wooden table and Frau Baumann, assisted by her daughter and daughter-in-law, served a simple but delicious lunch. The grandchildren, who'd been sneaking cookies and treats, showed little interest in the food, but no one seemed to care. And when they were done, the children bundled up and went outside to frolic in the freshly fallen snow.

"It feels almost enchanted," Adelaide whispered to Anton as they took coffee over to sit by the fireplace.

"Enchanted?" he repeated.

"Or magical, imaginary, idyllic? I can't find the right word. Like I'm living in a storybook or old movie. The way of life here in Montovia, well, it's like going back in time. It seems almost unreal."

"Not all of Montovia lives like this," he told her. "The Baumanns' farm is a very special place for sure, but Montovia has problems just like any place."

"Yes, I'm sure that must be true." She sighed. "I guess I'm just enjoying this sweet departure . . . while it lasts."

He held up his coffee mug in a toast. "Here's to this sweet departure. Happy Saint Nicholas Day."

She clinked her cup against his and returned his good tidings. A part of her was tempted to ask what, if anything, he'd heard from the police chief or his uncle. But at the same time, she didn't want to spoil this enchanted moment. This day felt like a rare and precious jewel. A day that couldn't happen very often . . . perhaps never again in her lifetime.

❄ ❄ ❄

The next day passed in a much quieter way. Adelaide started her day by helping Herr Baumann outside. She shoveled snow out of the chicken coop, fed the hens, and gathered nine eggs, some still warm. Herr Baumann's eyes lit up when he saw the eggs, explaining how hens produced fewer eggs in the winter months. "You bring luck, Princess Adelaide."

Adelaide forced a smile. She'd already told her hosts to simply call her Adelaide, but they seemed to delight in her discomfort at the title. A small price to pay for their warm hospitality, she supposed.

Following a hearty breakfast, Adelaide helped in the kitchen, and after they finished, she accepted Anton's invitation to take a walk in the snow. Dressed in jeans as well as her hostess's winter coat, gloves, and heavy boots, Adelaide felt more comfortable than she did in the fancier clothes she'd been wearing at the palace.

They had barely started on their walk when Anton heard his phone chiming. Pausing to check it, he frowned then excused himself to step out of Adelaide's earshot as he answered the call. Although curious, she occupied herself by cleaning snow off a stump, which was just the right height for a chair. She tucked the woolen coat under her and sat down to admire her surroundings. The countryside had been beautiful before the snow, but today, with the sun glistening in every direction, it was stunningly gorgeous. She almost wished she'd brought her phone to take photos, but instead she decided to etch these sights into her memory. Something to take with her . . . for always.

Hearing the crunching of footsteps, she turned to see Anton coming back. His expression, which she still had a hard time reading, was decidedly somber. Something was wrong.

"What is it?" she asked, concern present in her tone.

"The king." He paused. "Has passed."

"Passed?" She stood, grabbing Anton's arms. "You mean he's—he's dead?"

He simply nodded. As she collapsed into tears, he gathered her into his arms and held her. Stroking her back, he just let her cry.

Adelaide didn't know why losing her father hurt so much, but it did. Was it because it hadn't been that long since she'd lost her mother? Because her newfound relationship with her father had been so short-lived? Or was it because she had begun to feel such a genuine connection to him—only to have it severed prematurely?

"I'm so sorry for your loss," Anton said as she finally stepped away from him. "We knew he didn't have long to live, but no one expected him to pass so soon."

"I feel like I've been robbed." Her hands balled into fists. "I had such a short time with him. It feels unfair."

"I understand." He pursed his lips.

"I was barely getting to know him . . . and now he's gone." She felt fresh tears coming. Not wanting to show them, she started to walk quickly down the path. Anton stayed right with her, listening as she talked and ranted and speculated and processed until finally she was so tired and breathless, she had to pause. Feeling wetness on her cheeks, she attempted to wipe them with the rough woolen gloves.

"Here." Anton handed her a white handkerchief. "My mother taught me to always carry these, but I rarely see the need to use them."

She pressed the soft fabric to her cheeks, and smelling the freshness of it, she almost smiled. "Your mother sounds like a nice person."

"She is."

She held the damp handkerchief out to him. "Thank you."

"You keep it." His brown eyes glowed warmly as he looked at her, and for a moment, she thought he intended to kiss her . . . but she felt torn, the timing was all wrong. Then, feeling relieved that he didn't, she turned away. Tucking the damp handkerchief into a coat pocket, she took in a steadying breath and started to walk through the woods again, trudging step by step through the ankle-deep snow.

Her father was dead. She would never see him again. Not in this world. She tried to remember the last words he'd spoken to her, that he loved her. God be with her, he'd said. God's plan in God's time. It was almost as if he'd known . . . his health was failing . . . his life was ending.

Fifteen

After several minutes of mindlessly plodding through snow, Adelaide stopped. Realizing Anton was still with her, she turned to him. Feeling somewhat helpless and confused, she spoke out in a voice that sounded small and vulnerable and nothing like her usual confident self. "What now?"

His brow creased as he rubbed his chin. "You mean for this walk? Do you want to go on? We've already walked quite a ways. Are you tired?"

"Oh . . ." She glanced at the wooded hillside around her, realizing she'd probably been wandering like a befuddled nomad. "Are we lost?"

He grinned, turning to point at the clearly visible tracks in the snow behind them.

"Yes, of course." She slowly nodded. "Maybe we should go back."

As they retraced their steps, she asked Anton what would happen next. "I mean, in the kingdom. Now that King Max is gone, will Prince Georg be crowned king?"

"I don't think so. But I don't know for sure." He gave her a sideways glance. "I suppose that will depend on you."

"On me?"

"It was the king's dying wish that you would accept the throne, Adelaide. He left a letter specifying it."

She stopped in her tracks. "How can I possibly do that?"

He pursed his lips but said nothing. It felt like he was studying her closely, perhaps sizing her up, asking himself the same questions that were racing through her mind.

"What equips me to rule Montovia, Anton?" She glared at him with balled fists, like this was a fight. "I am not even a citizen here. I can hardly speak German. I don't really understand Montovia. I barely know your history and definitely don't understand your laws. I know absolutely nothing about ruling a country."

"I understand." He placed a hand on her shoulder and looked deeply into her eyes. "But your father must've believed in you, Adelaide. King Max was a very wise ruler. He must've felt you were fit to rule Montovia or he wouldn't have made it his dying wish. Because, more than anything, the king loved his country. And he loved you too. My uncle read me the letter over the phone. He wants you to read it as well. Your father called you a miracle. He believed God sent you to him just in the nick of time."

Once again, his gaze was so warm and intense, his face was so close . . . she expected a kiss. She closed her eyes, unsure of her emotions, but when his hand fell off her shoulder, she opened her eyes to see him stepping back with a solemn expression. For the second time she felt mixed emotions of disappointment and relief, and Anton simply shoved his hands into the pockets of his borrowed hunting jacket.

She started walking again, trying to think rationally. "This is just so unbelievable. I can barely wrap my head around it." She wanted to pour all this information through her normally analytical brain, wanted to sieve out the gurgling emotions that muddied the waters. But it was too much to process.

Montovia had lost its beloved king, but what did that really mean? What did it truly have to do with her?

Suddenly she remembered the queen's phone call and the implications of what she'd overheard. Images of her attempted abduction also flashed through her mind.

"What has become of Queen Johanna?" she asked. "Has the police chief questioned her yet? And what about my uncle Farcus? Did they find him?"

Anton seemed almost amused. "Now, you remind me of your father. Getting right down to business." As they continued trekking back to the farmhouse, Anton told her all that he knew about the situation. The queen's phone records had indeed revealed her connection to Steffen, as well as the suggestion that she was involved in some nefarious plots. Not only with the king's missing brother but perhaps with Adelaide as well. "Queen Johanna and Prince Georg, as well as a few others, are being held for questioning. So far, the queen is not talking, and Georg, although he's been more cooperative, doesn't seem to know much."

"Will it be in the news? An embarrassment for the kingdom?"

He shrugged. "The kingdom has a long history of embarrassments. The royal family will be the main topic of conversation for a while, but it's amazing how forgetful the public can be. Especially with all the other distractions."

"Distractions?"

"You know. The new princess, the missing prince, death of a king . . . they have plenty to talk about right now."

"I suppose that's a bit like the US and celebrities. But what about Prince Farcus being at the family villa outside of Vienna? Any update on that?"

Anton shook his head. "It was empty like before, but our investigators found evidence that he had been held there."

"Against his will?"

"So it seems."

"So you think the queen really intended to have my uncle killed?"

"That seems likely."

A cold chill rushed through her. "Is it possible Farcus is already dead?"

Anton sighed. "That is my uncle's fear. It would explain why the queen is being so tight-lipped."

"What a royal mess."

"You got that right."

By that evening, Adelaide was back at the palace. Although Albert had suggested she occupy the royal quarters, she insisted on remaining in her old suite. She knew Johanna and Georg would remain in custody until either a confession or sufficient evidence was secured so there was no worry that they would return, but Adelaide felt more comfortable in the smaller bedroom. After all, as she reminded Albert and Anton, she was still grieving her father. She needed time alone . . . to think.

Albert had read King Max's letter to her, after the three of them had a somber dinner in the royal dining room. Although it was touching to hear her father's confidence in her ability to lead Montovia, she was not convinced. It all seemed so bizarre and incomprehensible. She really wanted to talk to someone. Someone from her old life. Someone who knew her. She hadn't communicated with Maya for several days now and even then, only by text exchanges. She decided it was high time for a phone call. She calculated the time difference, then picked up her phone. It was afternoon for Maya, so she called.

Before Adelaide had a chance to speak, Maya started firing off questions about Anton. "I know you have feelings for the guy," she insisted. "So, tell me what's happening? How is he?"

"Anton is fine, Maya. But my father"—she paused to gather her composure—"the king, is dead."

Maya gasped. "Oh, honey, I'm so sorry. Are you doing okay?"

The sympathy tugged at Adelaide's heart, but she kept her voice even. "Yes. I'm okay. I mean, it's been hard. I barely got to know him, Maya. But he was a wonderful man. He would've been a good father. He loved me and I loved him."

"Then you should be thankful you went to visit him before it was too late. Will you stay on until Christmas now that he's gone?"

Now she spilled the story of her father's desire for her to rule Montovia. "Just saying those words out loud sounds so crazy. So . . . surreal."

"Wow!"

Disappointed in Maya's less-than-helpful response, Adelaide then told her about the queen's diabolical plan involving her missing uncle. "Prince Farcus would've been heir to the throne."

"No kidding! This sounds like a Masterpiece Theater movie."

"Come on, Maya. This is my life. And I really need to figure things out."

"So what do you want, Addie?"

She rubbed her hand over her eyes. "Want?"

"Yeah. What is your heart telling you? You talk about what they want from you, but what do you want?"

"Peace on earth?"

"Seriously. Your father wanted you to be queen. Is that what you want?"

"No, of course not. I've never wanted to be queen of anything. Especially not a whole country. Even if it is a small one."

"Then come home."

Adelaide considered this. Home? Where was home, really? With old Mrs. Crabtree and her cats?

"Okay, so you're not ready to come home yet. Tell me, where does Anton fit in? I was certain you had a serious crush on him."

Adelaide considered her words. Was she ready to admit to anyone, even her best friend, she had strong feelings for him? "Well, Anton has been pretty amazing."

"Aha, so you are crushing?"

"I don't know. Too much has been going on. It's hard to sort it all out."

"Okay, then. Back to Montovia. What are your feelings toward that teeny tiny country that's just a speck on the map?"

"Well, it seems bigger once you're here," she said in defense. "And to be honest, I really like Montovia. I mean, I actually pretty much *love* it. It's not perfect, but it's just really quaint and sweet."

"Could you live there?"

She carefully considered this. "I think maybe I could . . . under the right circumstances."

"As the queen?"

Adelaide let out a loud sigh. "I just don't see myself as queen material, Maya. I'm not a ruler."

"But you were studying law, and you're very intelligent. As your best friend I know you're highly opinionated and extremely strong-willed. You never let anyone walk over you. And yet you're kindhearted—most of the time. If you ask me, those all seem like good qualities for a ruler."

"Thanks. That's sweet of you to say that."

"Well, it's all true, *Queen* Adelaide." Maya laughed. "I just cannot imagine you strutting around in a long purple robe with a crown on your head. Would people have to bow down and call you 'your majesty'?"

"Very funny. For your information it doesn't work that way. I never saw my father in a robe or a crown. In fact, he was very practical and down-to-earth. The people called him King Max, and those close to him just called him Max." She felt a wave of sentiment wash over her. "He was a good guy, Maya."

"Yeah, I get that. And he wanted you to follow in his footsteps."

"Yes . . . that's the hard part. I mean, I do want to honor my father. According to Albert—he's been my main advisor—it's important to Montovia's stability that someone take the throne as soon as possible. And since I'm King Max's daughter—"

"I think you want to do this," Maya cut her off.

"I guess I just feel sort of responsible, you know? Like this sweet country needs me."

"Does that feel good? Being needed like that?"

Adelaide considered this. "You know, it sort of does."

"For the record, I think you'd make a good queen, Addie."

"Thanks."

"So, when do I get to come visit?" Maya asked eagerly.

"Come for Christmas," Adelaide urged. "Maybe I can pay your way. I could tell them I need you here as an advisor or a counselor."

"Seriously? My passport is good."

"I'll ask and get back to you."

"So, you really plan to do it? You'll let them crown you queen?"

"I don't know. I promised to prayerfully consider it. That's what I'll be doing tonight. Would you keep me in your prayers too?"

"Absolutely. Keep me in the loop. Let me know what you decide and when I can come visit."

Adelaide promised to do that. As soon as she hung up the phone, she actually got down on her knees and begged God to show her his will. *God's plan in God's time.*

After a restless night of weighing the pros and cons of this life-changing decision, she knew what she needed to do. It wouldn't be easy, but she would take the throne for her father and the country he loved. She would accept the crown and serve Montovia. She believed it was greater to serve than to be served. And if she found happiness—maybe even love—in the process, it would all be worth it. She met with Albert and the royal councilors to let them know that if they all agreed it was the best plan, she was ready to serve Montovia as queen. They all thanked and congratulated her, and the wheels were set in motion to hold the king's funeral service Sunday morning and a solemn coronation the same afternoon. Parliament would be notified, and press releases would be sent out immediately.

After the deputy ministers left, Albert remained behind to update her on Johanna. She noticed he no longer referred to her as Queen Johanna. "We are preparing a deal for her and Georg," he said. "Whether or not she makes a full confession, the police chief believes there is enough evidence to persuade her that her role in the royal family is terminated."

"What is the evidence?" she asked, taking on the role of defense attorney. Albert listed off the various items in the case they were building against Johanna. It sounded reasonable . . . and sad.

"Georg even helped by admitting his mother has been having an affair with Steffen for several years."

"My poor father." She shook her head. "I wonder if he knew."

"It would explain the coolness in their relationship." Albert sighed. "Very unfortunate."

"Although I have no warm feelings toward Johanna, I would want her to be dealt with fairly."

"We plan to offer her and her son permanent exile from Montovia."

"Will she accept it?"

"According to Montovian law, we could imprison her . . . or worse." He shook his head grimly. "I think she will accept our terms."

"Well, please keep me apprised," she told him.

He smiled. "You already sound like a queen."

"I hope so. I really don't know how this will go, but I want my father to be proud of me. I'm doing this for him." She held her chin higher. "And for Montovia. I have really grown to love this country. I want to serve it the best I can."

"It will do the people good to know this. A country can suffer during a shift of power."

"I wondered about that. After all, some will see me as an outsider."

"That's true. But the majority of citizens loved their king. When they read his letter, which will be included in the press release, they will probably be relieved. Most of them, anyway."

"I assume Johanna and Georg had some devoted followers too."

He nodded. "You saw what happened at the Krampus party."

She cringed at the memory.

"There will undoubtedly be some opposition to you. We will do our best to manage it."

"Will the queen's exile be public knowledge?"

"It will be handled most diplomatically."

"Well, do please keep me informed, Albert."

He tipped his head. "I will. You will have a busy day ahead of you. Your staff will be preparing for Sunday's ceremonies, and you will have some advisors helping you to understand your role."

She thanked him, then vaguely wondered how the queen of Montovia was supposed to navigate a romantic relationship. She knew the queen of England's husband had been Prince Philip, but the queen was the true monarch. How would Anton Balazs feel about being called Prince Anton? Perhaps she was letting her imagination run away with her. Best to keep focused on the task at hand. Besides, she suspected, a monarch's life was probably a bit of a lonely one.

CHAPTER

Sixteen

A delaide didn't think it was her imagination that her relationship with Anton had seemed to change over-night. Instead of feeling like her friend, he felt more like a royal advisor on assignment. The warmth she'd enjoyed before had been replaced with an efficient businesslike attitude. Certainly, Anton was helpful, but he was clearly just doing his job. And by the end of the next day, he'd convinced her that her new personal assistant, a tall blond woman named Lina, would take over where he left off.

Adelaide had no complaints about her new assistant. Lina spoke perfect English and was well educated, and as the daughter of a deputy minister, she was devoted to her homeland. Lina had been handling PR for the palace and Parliament for the last ten years. She was dedicated to her career and now, it seemed, to Adelaide as well. A perfect choice for the queen's personal assistant. But was that any excuse for the coolness Adelaide now received from Anton?

And so, as Anton was telling Adelaide good night on the eve of her father's funeral and her coronation, she decided to cut to the chase and question him. "I feel like you're stepping away from your friendship with me," she said as they lingered in the doorway of the royal family's living quarters. "Is that right?"

His eyes looked cloudy, but he nodded. "As always, you are perceptive."

She reached for his hand. "But you've been such a good friend, Anton. I hate to think I'm losing you."

He squeezed her hand, then released it. "It's not proper for me to remain a close friend, Adelaide. Tomorrow I will address you as queen. You have Lina to assist you with the things I once helped with. She is highly qualified and well connected to the palace staff."

"I can see that. And I like her. But you have been my friend and confidante. I hate to lose that."

He stood straighter. "I understand. But it's unavoidable. My uncle has made it clear that I am to step back. Already there has been talk that I am overly involved with you. Besides that, I suspect I have neglected my own province responsibilities. Plus, with the Christmas holidays upon us"—he cleared his throat—"I need to spend more time with my family."

His excuses had fallen flat on her ears until he mentioned his family. For some reason, that filled her with an unexpected and overwhelming loneliness. Where was her family? How would she spend her Christmas? She remembered the cheery holiday warmth at the Baumanns' home. Would they consider hosting her during the holidays? Probably not. Now that she was about to become queen, everything changed. The lonely life of a monarch—it was beginning.

"Well, then, I thank you, Herr Balazs," she said politely. "For all you have done since I arrived here. I will always appreciate your kindness and your help." She held her head high, hoping he wouldn't notice the glistening of tears in her eyes. "Gute nacht." And then she closed the door.

The funeral for King Maximillian V was held in the cathedral and was well attended, with standing room only. Respectably dressed in a charcoal gray dress with a single string of pearls, Adelaide took her place in the front row with Lina on one side and Albert on the other. By now the exile of the queen and her son was fairly common knowledge in the kingdom. Rumors, not far from the truth, were circulating. And other than a few outspoken individuals, no one seemed overly concerned about the recent royal changes. Like Anton had told her, people moved on quickly.

Adelaide listened intently to the service. Although it was long, the words said were touching, and the tears shed seemed genuine. King Max had been a devoted ruler. He'd been well loved and would be dearly missed. Adelaide had big shoes to fill.

She knew the palace's press releases about the new queen had gone out the night before. According to Albert, who joined her for a quiet luncheon and was now acting as her official advisor, there had been a few opponents, protesting Adelaide's right to wear the crown.

"It's not unexpected," Albert explained.

"Is it because my parents weren't married?"

He waved a hand. "The protestors may use that as an excuse, but it isn't the first time this has happened in Montovia."

She tilted her head to the side in confusion. "What do you mean?"

"Your great-grandfather was born under similar circumstances, and he ruled without objection."

"I didn't know that."

"There's no need to worry. We are dealing with it."

"How?" she persisted.

"As you know, we published the king's final letter. Also, we've released quotes from our lawbooks, stating succession rules, which are supported by Parliament. And we've reminded people about your great-grandfather."

"You think that's enough."

He nodded firmly. "As King Max's daughter, you are the legitimate heir, Adelaide."

The word *legitimate* rang false in her ears, but she kept her thoughts to herself. "What about my father's adoption of Prince Georg?"

"Georg doesn't have the bloodlines that you have."

"That's true. But Johanna and Georg still have some citizen support. I suspect those are the ones who will cause trouble."

"We are prepared to fully expose Johanna's indiscretions if necessary. We prefer that she make a full public confession, but if she refuses, we will share a press release explaining why she and her son have no claim to the throne."

"So, she's still giving you the silent treatment?"

"She is a stubborn, prideful, and selfish woman."

Adelaide just nodded. This was not news to her.

"So, are you ready for the coronation this afternoon?" he asked brightly.

"I'll admit that my head is spinning some."

"We regret that so much is thrust upon you so suddenly, but it is how things are done here. Do you have all you need for the ceremony? Are you fully prepared?"

"Lina has been an excellent coach. She has chosen my gowns and instructed me on every step, but I know she still wants to go over it with me again."

"Lina is a treasure."

"I agree." Adelaide tried not to compare her new assistant to Anton. It wasn't fair. Instead, she checked the clock. "In fact, I'm due to meet with her in ten minutes."

"I will see you at the ceremony." Albert clasped her hand. "Your father would be very proud of you, Princess Adelaide. I believe he will be watching today." He glanced upward. "And cheering!"

"I hope so." Adelaide attempted a smile to cover her nerves.

Although she'd felt God's peace in all this, she still had questions and concerns. But she reminded herself, *God's plan in God's time*. She could live only one day—perhaps only one moment—at a time.

Other than a motley handful of protestors outside of the cathedral, the coronation ceremony had started off smoothly. Adelaide peeked out the door of the side room where she and Lina waited. To her relief, there was only a small group in attendance. According to Lina, this was the acceptable expectation for a coronation held on the same day as a royal funeral. It was more respectful.

"It's almost time." Lina adjusted the sash of the simple white gown she'd chosen for Adelaide's coronation. Adelaide had never been so meticulously dressed and vaguely wondered if this was how a bride felt before her wedding day . . . Not that she would ever know. What man in his right mind would want to marry a ruling queen? She doubted that many Prince Philips remained in the modern world.

As the prelude to the Montovian national anthem began, Lina prompted Adelaide to make her entrance. Taking in a deep, calming breath, Adelaide stepped out. Waiting for her was the general of the small Montovian army, in full formal dress. It was the general's duty to protect Adelaide and to usher her to the altar where Prime Minister Albert Kovacs would guide her in repeating her vows to the kingdom. Her first step was to publicly accept Montovian citizenship. Next, she took her vows as the ruler. As she repeated Albert's words, she reminded herself that her primary purpose as queen was to serve the people, not to be served by them. As the crown was placed on her head, Adelaide wondered if her father really was watching. She hoped he was smiling—or cheering, as Albert had imagined.

That evening, the palace was full. Food and drink flowed freely, and the ballroom floor was opened for dancing. The musicians, selected by Queen Adelaide with Lina's help, were well suited for respectable dancing—nothing like the music at the Krampus party. For this celebration ceremony, Queen Adelaide wore a pale lavender taffeta gown with a fitted bodice and a full flowing skirt that swooshed when she walked. Again, it had been picked by Lina. Adelaide had opted for the diamond necklace her father had given her. This piece, along with the crown pinned securely on her head, actually did make her feel rather queenly.

Adelaide was greeted by various dignitaries. She danced with some of them, but mostly she sat at the royal table with Lina and Albert flanking her. The two royal councilors and their wives were seated nearby as well. With a few prompts from Lina, Adelaide attempted to make proper conversation but wished this awkward evening would end early.

Meanwhile, Anton and other members of Parliament, along with their wives or dates, were seated at surrounding tables. Many of the couples seemed to be enjoying the festivities. Adelaide had to control herself from glancing at Anton, hoping he might ask for a dance. At least, from what she could see, he didn't have a date.

After about an hour, Anton actually came her way. Her hopes rose in the anticipation he would invite her to dance, but instead he simply greeted and congratulated her, then turned to Lina and invited her to dance. Adelaide couldn't deny they made a handsome couple, but she wished she was the one in his arms—and that the crown weighing heavy on her head was only a dream. But it was real. And the pins holding the headpiece in place were starting to itch. But it seemed unqueenly to scratch one's head in public. Or maybe she was making too much of this. She took in a deep breath and thought about her father. Had he ever felt like this?

For the next week, Queen Adelaide stayed moderately busy. Part of her time was spent being tutored by Albert on all things Montovian and coached by Lina on how to dress and behave at the various social invitations she received on a daily basis. Lina always accompanied her to the social engagements, and Adelaide played her role to the best of her ability. But after a while, she began to suspect she was more of a figurehead than anything else.

The fact she was a woman only seemed to water down her leadership role. She didn't want to be judgmental, but visiting baby nurseries, women's church groups, and pie socials didn't hold great appeal to someone who'd hoped to practice law someday. But hopefully, in time, she would change Montovia's backward attitude toward women.

Early in her second week, she'd made another uncomfortable observation. It seemed clear that a number of outspoken Montovian citizens severely questioned her authority and ability to rule. To be fair, those were the same concerns she'd originally harbored. She couldn't deny being an American or her lack of leadership training or her inability to speak German with her compatriots, but she took exception to their insinuation that being female was a critical shortcoming. She was ready to go to the mat for that one!

But her harshest criticism by far, and the hardest thing to ignore, was their accusation that she was *illegitimately* born and therefore an *illegitimate* claim to the throne. Thankfully only a handful of citizens held that view, and most were likely old friends of Johanna, but the insinuations still stung. She couldn't deny that her mother had never married King Max. But what did they expect her to do about that now? And why were they rubbing her nose in it?

Albert urged her to put these aggravations behind her, but

thanks to an opinionated journalist, it was difficult. Plus, there were some news sources who enjoyed putting her down for being a "frivolous woman." And, really, she couldn't blame them for some negative observations. She felt a bit foolish getting all dressed up and attending silly functions she had no interest in—and she was tired of tea and pastries! She'd even pleaded with Albert to let her take on more leadership responsibilities in hopes that she might prove herself as worthy. But he assured her that was to come later. After the holidays.

"The Christmas season is more for socializing than governing," he explained as they prepared to leave for a tea he'd offered to accompany her to . . . after she'd complained it was her fifth tea in as many days. "This slow spell is rather fortuitous, Queen Adelaide." He helped her into the limousine. "It is your opportunity to build important relationships. The season will pass soon enough. Do not worry. There will be plenty for you to do after the new year."

As he slid into the back seat, his phone chimed. "The police chief sent a message," he told her as he read the text. "He wants me to call him immediately." He held up his phone. "Do you mind?"

"Not at all." She waved a dismissive hand. It was still odd to have people asking her permission to do ordinary things. Would she ever get used to this? She gazed out the window as they passed through the village, trying not to eavesdrop too much as Albert talked to the chief. He said *ja* and *nein* a few times, followed by several excited exclamations that suggested something big was going on. She turned to watch him, knowing if this was police business, it could involve something dangerous.

By now she knew that Johanna and Georg and Steffen, as well as a few others, had exited the country to avoid legal charges. She'd heard they were all relocating to Argentina. She doubted this phone call was related to any of them, but there was such an air of urgency about it, she was eager to hear what had happened. Finally, Albert hung up and turned to her with a serious look.

"Queen Adelaide, I have news." His expression was grim.

"Bad news?" she asked.

"It depends." He took in a deep breath, slowly exhaling as if to organize his words. "Your uncle. He is alive."

"Prince Farcus?" She sat up straighter. "Tell me everything!"

"It seems that Steffen relocated Prince Farcus when Johanna was taken into custody. That's the reason we didn't find him in Vienna. Johanna probably directed this, hoping to get out of the country before it all blew up. Farcus had been kept in a summer vacation home where a caretaker was paid to hold him indefinitely. When payments ceased, your uncle was released. He just contacted the chief this morning."

"Really?" She felt a rush of hope. "Is he okay?"

"Other than being malnourished and rather unkempt, he is fine."

"That is wonderful news. Will he return to Montovia?"

"He will arrive at the palace tomorrow. Of course, we will keep this quiet for now."

"Why quiet?"

"It will need to be handled very carefully."

"I see . . ." She tried to discern why he seemed so concerned. "This seems like something to celebrate though. Prince Farcus is alive. He is coming home."

Albert leaned toward her with a furrowed brow. "Do you fully understand what this means, Queen Adelaide?"

"Yes. It means Prince Farcus, as second-born son to my grandfather, King Maximillian IV, is the legal heir to the throne. Ahead of me."

"That's right." He exhaled, clearly relieved.

"Do you think he will make a good king?" she asked.

Albert's brow creased slightly. "I hope so."

Now she felt a wave of concern, both for her father's sake as well as Montovia's. "What if he turns out to be a bad king?" she whispered.

Albert rubbed his chin with a thoughtful expression. "There is always that possibility . . . with any ruler. It's why we have Parliament and prime ministers." His phone was chiming again and while he checked it, she considered the situation. At the moment, she was queen. But what did that really mean? Even if Farcus proved a terrible ruler, it was still out of her hands. There would be nothing she could do to prevent anything. Like her father told her, *God's plan in God's time.* She'd have to wait to see how God's plan would turn out.

The remainder of Queen Adelaide's Advent season social obligations were canceled. For which she was grateful! The excuse given was that the queen needed time to prepare for Christmas, which was now just five days away. The real reason was that Prince Farcus, sneaked into the palace under cover, would now be in meetings with the prime ministers and Adelaide. All agreed this had to be handled extremely carefully.

Adelaide wanted to spend as much time as possible with her uncle in hopes of getting better acquainted. Oh, she knew that whichever way this went was out of her hands, but in respect for her father, she wanted to do her best to make a good connection with his brother.

It wasn't until Prince Farcus's second day in the palace, after a day of food and rest and making himself at home in the royal quarters, that he was ready to meet the reigning queen. Thanks to Albert, Farcus had been brought up to speed on the strange happenings since his abduction two months before.

"I am very pleased to meet you, *Queen* Adelaide." His eyes twinkled as he tipped his head toward her, clasping her hand in his. "I did not know I had a niece. Und such a lovely one too."

"Thank you. I'm so relieved that you made it safely home."

"Are you?" His brow creased as if he doubted this.

She took a seat by the fireplace in the royal family living room. "Of course I am relieved." She smiled at him. "You are my uncle. My father's brother. I am very pleased to have you safely home."

"You have been queen for . . . not even two weeks?" He sat across from her with a puzzled expression. "Und you are *pleased* to see me?"

"It was never my intention to be queen. I came here to meet my father and, well, I'm sure you've heard the whole tale by now."

He slowly shook his head as if he, too, was still processing it. "What a tale it is."

"You must have quite a story to tell yourself. I've heard some of it already." She studied him. In many ways he seemed a younger version of King Max. Tall, thin, straight nose, high hairline, dark brown hair. But his eyes, instead of green, were golden.

"Ja. I gave up hope."

"How sad." She wanted more details. "So, I heard that Johanna's friend Steffen took you captive. Is that right?"

"Ja. I was surprised to see Steffen at Vienna train station. I thought happy coincidence. Steffen bought me eines beer." He held up one finger. "Und that is all I remember. I woke in damp, dark wine cellar. In my own family villa! But I did not know that."

"Were you frightened?"

"At first, I expected to be killed. When that did not happen, I had time to think. I knew Steffen and Johanna were involved. I thought that must be motive. To keep me from informing my brother of their illicit plans."

"Perhaps that was part of it." Adelaide considered the possibility. "Although I'm sure it had more to do with Georg inheriting the throne. Johanna wanted to help rule."

"Ja. But you came and spoiled that plan." He smiled. "That was gut."

For a long moment the room was silent except for the crackling of the fire. Adelaide still had questions for her uncle, but she wasn't sure how to continue.

"Were you treated badly when you were locked up?" she finally asked.

"The food was furchtbar—awful! Often they forgot to feed me at all." He winked. "At least I had wine."

"That was convenient. Still, it must've been horrible."

"Ja, ja. The worst was isolation. Very lonely. Und no windows, no clocks. I know not how many days pass. It was like years. Only eight weeks, ja. For me, a lifetime."

"I can't even imagine."

"Ja, it was bad. But also gut."

"Good?" Had she misheard him?

"Time. Time was all I had. Time to think. Time to remember my parents. Time to think of my brother. Good King Max." His eyes got misty. "I am so sorry he is gone. So much have I missed."

"He was a very good man."

"Ja. Und a very good king."

"He was so worried for you. I think he believed you were dead. That was the only explanation we had for your absence."

"Und now he is dead. I miss him." He touched his chest. "Inside."

"You say he was a very good king, Prince Farcus, and I agree with you. Even though I didn't know my father that long, I know how much he loved his country and his people."

"Ja, that is for certain." Farcus nodded.

"How about you? Do you feel the same way?"

"Do you know meaning of my name? Farcus?"

She shook her head.

"It is Hungarian. From my mutter's ancestor. Farcus means wolf."

"Wolf?"

"Ja. Some think wolf is bad—the wolf is a thief und evil. Others think the wolf strong und brave und loyal."

"What do you think? What kind of wolf are you?"

He looked directly into her eyes. "If you ask me before, I would not know. I would give no good answer."

"But now?" she pressed.

"I am strong und brave wolf. And loyal."

"And is that how you would act as king?" she asked. "Strong and brave and loyal?"

"Ja. I would be strong und brave und loyal. I love Montovia. I love the people." He nodded vigorously, then smiled. "But I think I needed to be locked up to know this."

She smiled back at him. "And you really do want to be king?"

"Ja." His smile faded. "Und you will not be sad, Queen Adelaide? You must give up the crown? For me?"

"I am glad to give it up." And for the most part she was glad, but a small part of her felt sad too. She had wanted to serve the people of Montovia. But she'd never really gotten the chance. It had seemed more like they'd been serving her. Always giving her flowers and the seat of honor, serving her tea, performing for her, treating her like a celebrity. That hadn't been what she'd expected or wanted. But maybe she'd just gotten it all wrong. Or maybe she had simply been a placeholder.

Seventeen

Somehow word leaked out that Prince Farcus had returned and, rather than let the press run wild with false accounts or premature presumptions, Adelaide called a royal press conference for the following afternoon. More than anything she wanted this to be a smooth transition . . . for everyone. The prime ministers had recommended wrapping it all up before Christmas. So, standing at the foot of the palace stairs, Queen Adelaide prepared to make the official announcement.

"I am greatly relieved to tell you my uncle, Prince Farcus, is alive and well and ready to take the throne." She waited for the reporters to react, holding her head high as several cameras recorded her. "I have only been your temporary queen," she continued, "and I have been honored to represent my father in my efforts to serve Montovia, even for such a short reign. Now I will gladly pass the crown on to my uncle. I am proud to stand by his side in this transition. The ceremony is scheduled for four o'clock on Christmas Eve. Following the coronation will be a festive celebration right here in the palace. It will be a happy day for everyone."

She paused and waited for questions. Several eager hands rose, and Adelaide chose a young reporter to her left.

"Prince Farcus has been missing for weeks. Is he the best royal to rule Montovia?" he asked, pointing his recording device in her direction.

"I do believe he is the best royal to rule. Prince Farcus was not responsible for his absence, and we do not hold that against him. I believe my uncle will serve our country to the best of his ability."

"Will you remain in Montovia?" another reporter shouted.

She smiled but decided to answer vaguely. "I do plan to remain through the holidays. In fact, a friend of mine from America is about to join me here." She wondered if Maya's plane had touched down in Vienna yet. She was due to the palace by six.

"Is your American friend a *man*?" a young woman called out in a teasing tone. "Do we hear wedding bells perhaps?"

"No," Adelaide answered firmly. "It is my best friend from childhood. She wants to spend Christmas with me."

"But will you remain here *after* Christmas, Queen Adelaide? Or will you return to your homeland?" The reporter's tone was insistent. He wanted an answer.

She wondered about the wording. "I feel that Montovia *is* my homeland. I love this country."

"Yes, but will you go back to America?" a woman called out.

Adelaide thought hard. "I cannot say for sure what I will do. If there is reason for me to remain in Montovia, if I can be of help to my uncle, I would like to stay. But I cannot give a firm answer right now. All I can say is what my father used to tell me. *God's plan in God's time.* I must leave it at that. Thank you." She smiled and turned to Lina, who was waiting behind her. "Let's go," she whispered.

"Wait!" someone yelled out. "One more question!"

She turned at the familiar voice. It was actually Anton, standing amid the throng of reporters. She stepped back up to the microphone. "Yes? Your question, sir?"

"Thank you." He nodded, his brown eyes twinkling. "If you had a very good reason to remain in Montovia, would you stay, Queen Adelaide?"

"If it were a *very* good reason, I would be pleased to remain." She waited a moment, trying not to appear as flustered as she felt. "Is that all?"

"Not quite." He grinned. "Will there be any dancing at the Christmas Eve festivities following the coronation?"

"Absolutely," she assured him. "Any more questions?" She glanced across the amused crowd, prepared to make a quick getaway.

"One more, Queen Adelaide." Anton waved his hand like an eager first grader. "Will the queen save a dance for me?"

The reporters chortled, some even made sly remarks, and a few elbowed Anton, but Adelaide's fixed smile remained steady. "I would be honored to dance with you, sir. Thank you very much, everyone. Have a good evening." She waved to the crowd, hoping the roses in her cheeks weren't too noticeable as she hurried to rejoin Lina.

"What was Anton doing?" Lina whispered as they headed up the palace stairs as well-wishes were called out behind them.

"I don't know." Adelaide couldn't help but giggle. "I think he wanted to put me on the spot."

Lina laughed. "I think he wanted more than that."

Because Prince Farcus was having a dinner meeting with the prime ministers, Adelaide arranged to have dinner privately with Maya. She'd already given her friend the full tour and, naturally, Maya was blown away by all of it.

"I can't believe you're giving this all up," Maya said as they were served. "How can you stand to leave it all behind?"

"Like I already told you, being queen was turning out to be

a lonely job. More attention was paid to my wardrobe than my mind."

"And what a wardrobe." Maya forked into her pheasant. "Do you get to keep any of it?"

"I suppose I will keep the clothes, but the jewels and the furs . . . I'm not so sure. In fact, I'd rather not keep them. They're more fit for a queen."

"But your uncle has no wife." Maya's eyes lit up. "Hey, do I get to meet him?"

Adelaide laughed. "Of course, you'll meet him. But I don't think you're his type. Plus, he's a little old for you."

"Yeah, and besides, I met this new guy. Eric." Maya sighed as she helped herself to another roll. "He was subbing at my school after Thanksgiving. He was acting interested and even asked me about my Christmas plans."

"You mean I've taken you away from—"

"No, no. It's okay." Maya buttered her roll. "I told him where I was going and he was so interested, I promised to tell him all about it when I get home."

"Well, thank you for coming. I was so lonely, and you're the closest thing to family I have anymore." Adelaide picked up her water goblet.

"What about your uncle? He's family."

"That's true. But I barely know him."

"Lina seems nice. Isn't she sort of like family?"

"Sort of, but she was working as my assistant."

"Okay, then, what about Anton?"

Adelaide smiled. "I haven't had a real conversation with him since I was crowned."

"Based on what you said he did at your press conference, I'll bet that's about to change."

For the rest of the evening, it was just Adelaide and Maya, enjoying what felt like an old-time sleepover—just in a royal palace. It was well past midnight when they parted ways to go to bed. Adelaide had moved back to her previous suite, leaving the royal chambers to Farcus. Maya was happily occupying what had previously been Georg's suite. The plan was to sleep in tomorrow, and then Adelaide would show Maya the village and do some last-minute Christmas shopping.

On the morning of Christmas Eve, Adelaide prepared herself for her last day as queen of Montovia. It started with a special Christmas church service. Accompanied by Lina and Maya, Adelaide was conservatively outfitted in her green velveteen dress and a single strand of pearls. This was topped with the Russian sable coat, and because there was still snow, she wore her tall black boots.

"You look so regal," Maya said as they rode the short distance to the coronation in the limousine. "You sure you won't miss all this?"

Adelaide shook her head. "I'm ready for freedom."

"But being queen should feel like freedom." Maya still didn't get it. "You have everything you could possibly want. Clothes, cars, furs, jewels, the palace, and—"

"They're not really mine," Adelaide tried to explain again. "They belong to the royal family. I'm just temporarily using them to represent the kingdom." She glanced to Lina. "Isn't that right?"

Lina smiled. "For such a short reign, you do seem to understand. Perhaps better than most royals."

"Meaning royals are entitled?" Maya questioned

"I suppose those who grow up with privileges do tend to be entitled," Lina responded.

"So, wouldn't that describe Prince Farcus?" Maya challenged them. "He grew up as a prince."

"Yes, but his situation was a little different." Adelaide pulled the sable coat more snugly around her neck. "Prince Farcus was so much younger than my father, he didn't get much of the limelight. Most of it was focused on his brother. I think my uncle thought of himself as sort of the black sheep." She looked to Lina. "Is that how you perceived him?"

"Maybe. I know he wasn't very popular with the people." Lina's expression was thoughtful. "I think perhaps he was misunderstood."

"Do you know him well?" Maya pointed to Lina.

"Well enough." Lina tugged on one of her leather gloves.

"Why do you think he never married?" Maya persisted. "Isn't he in his forties?"

"He's forty-five," Lina said. "And he's had a number of women in his life, but for some reason he's never settled down."

"A confirmed bachelor?" Maya patted a stray strand of hair back into place.

"I hope not." Adelaide felt a little uneasy about Maya's pushy questioning, but understood her curiosity. "I think a king or a queen needs a partner. It can be pretty lonely."

Maya nudged Lina with her elbow. "What about her?"

"Maya!" Adelaide couldn't help but laugh, but she tossed her friend a warning look. "I don't think Lina needs a matchmaker."

But Maya looked determined, still eying Lina. "Is it that you don't like Prince Farcus? Or is he too old for you?"

"Well, he is five years older." Lina fiddled with the latch on her evening bag. "But that's not much."

"And you seem like you'd make a good queen," Maya continued.

"Maya," Adelaide put an edge into her voice. "Stop needling Lina."

"It's all right." Lina smiled at Maya. "To be honest, I used to admire the prince . . . from a distance."

"Aha!" Maya pointed to Adelaide. "See, I was onto something, and you didn't even know it."

Thankfully, they reached the cathedral, and all talk of Lina and Farcus was set aside. Still, Adelaide couldn't help but wonder if Maya really had been onto something. She also wondered if she, as a member of the royal family, might be able to give this theory a few gentle nudges. Her uncle could do far worse than Lina. And yet, she reminded herself, a marriage for love was far better than one of convenience.

Before and during the coronation, Adelaide made sure to keep Lina nearby. Partly because she really needed her help and partly as a way to bring her to her uncle's attention. The coronation ceremony went off just as smoothly and was very similar to the one two weeks ago. Except that it was Adelaide who was allowed to crown her uncle King Farcus.

Though she would probably never admit it, the ceremony was bittersweet. She was glad to be free of the royal responsibilities and the loneliness, but a part of her had hoped to use the crown to really serve the people of Montovia and to make her father proud. Her extremely short reign had come to an abrupt end.

As she stood on the sidelines, listening to the choir singing before King Farcus made his first speech, she looked up to where sun was streaming through the stained glass window and imagined her father smiling down on her. It was almost as if she could really feel him—like his hand was on her shoulder with the comforting assurance that she'd pleased him. *God's plan in God's time.* Two weeks had been exactly right.

Adelaide felt like she was floating as she and Maya went down to the ballroom for the Christmas Eve party and coronation celebration. She had never felt so free and unburdened since arriving at Montovia. It was as if all the heaviness had been lifted, and she was able to simply enjoy herself. Tonight she wore an emerald green satin gown. This, too, had been selected by Lina, whose fashion sense was so flawless, Adelaide wondered if she'd be able to dress without her. The stylish gown, Maya had pointed out, matched Adelaide's eyes almost perfectly. Adelaide also wore the diamond necklace, which King Farcus had told her belonged to her. As well as the fur coat.

"Those were gifts from your father. You *must* keep them!" her uncle had finally proclaimed as they went over final loose ends together. King Farcus still wanted to know her plans for the future. He'd encouraged her to remain in Montovia and make it her home, but as she told him and everyone—including Maya, who asked hourly—she wasn't sure where her home was anymore.

"You look beautiful," she told Maya as they went down the palace stairs to the first floor.

"Thanks to Lina." Maya ran a hand down her burgundy lace skirt. "That woman is amazing. A fashionista with a brain."

"Speaking of Lina, you remember the plan for when we enter the ballroom?" Adelaide asked under her breath.

"Yeah. I'll go sit by Albert and his wife while you and your uncle cut the rug."

Adelaide frowned. "Cut the rug?"

"That's what my grandpa calls dancing."

Adelaide smiled as they entered the ballroom. Filled with formally attired guests, the room smelled of enticing food, and quiet music played from the orchestra ensemble. The celebration was ready to begin. As planned, King Farcus, who was seated at the royal table, would stand to welcome Princess Adelaide to the party. The ensemble would play the national anthem with King Farcus saluting the flag and Princess Adelaide a few feet behind him. Then the ensemble would start to play

"The Royal Waltz," and Adelaide would dance with the king. This had been Lina's idea, and Albert had heartily agreed. Just one more way to reassure everyone that this had been a peaceful and congenial transfer of power.

After their dance ended, King Farcus and Princess Adelaide were expected to choose new partners, and the dance floor would be open to all. At Adelaide's suggestion, her uncle would invite Lina to dance. Secretly, Adelaide hoped to spy Anton and ask him to join her. However, as she and Farcus twirled about the floor, she discreetly surveyed the guests but didn't see Anton anywhere. Her heart sank. Was he even here?

The waltz ended, Farcus bowed, and the princess curtsied as the crowd cheered. While the musicians played a brief interlude, the two royals set off to find their next partners. Lina, as instructed, was waiting nearby, looking glamorous in a silvery blue gown. She took the king's hand with a smile on her face. Adelaide, feeling a bit lost, gave up on Anton and decided to ask Albert instead. She was halfway to him when she felt a gentle tap on her shoulder. Turning around, she felt her face light up at the sight of Anton. Looking incredibly handsome in his formal attire, he smiled as he took a deep bow.

"May I have this dance?" he asked, extending his hand to her.

Adelaide didn't miss the amused twitters of some of the onlookers—as if they were privy to this little joke. Ignoring them, she smiled. "Of course."

The ensemble started to play "The Blue Danube," and Anton took her into his arms. Suddenly they were waltzing and happily whirling around the ballroom as other couples, the royal counselors, and Parliament members joined them. Not for the first time since coming to Montovia, Adelaide was grateful for the classical dancing lessons her mother had forced her to take as a preadolescent. And for a brief happy moment, she imagined her beautiful mother and handsome father, both whole and well, energetically waltzing together in heaven right now. The image was so sweet that her smile grew even bigger.

After the number ended, Anton led her from the dance floor. "I'm sorry I was late," he said as they strolled along the sidelines.

"I'm just glad you made it." She kept her arm looped in his as he led them out into the main hall, stopping to admire the enormous Christmas tree with its colorful lights and decorations.

"I got distracted by my sister at her restaurant."

"How is Elsa?"

"She's fine. I was helping her to prepare for a little Christmas Eve party she is hosting at her restaurant. She wants me to invite you."

"Tonight? Another party?"

"Yes. It will begin around nine. Just an intimate gathering. Good food and drink, singing and merrymaking."

"Interesting. Who will be there?"

"Elsa, her husband, my parents, a few others. My family always celebrates Christmas Eve together. Usually at our parents' home, but since Uncle Albert and a few others had to be at the palace, well, Elsa offered her restaurant for *after* the party. It'll be a family thing."

"A family thing?" She paused in front of the nativity she'd set up a few weeks ago. She leaned over and straightened some of the straw in the manger, making baby Jesus more comfortable.

"Yes. Aunts, uncles, cousins . . . just a small, happy crowd. And you must bring your American friend. And anyone else for that matter."

"What about my uncle?" she asked with uncertainty.

He laughed. "The king is most welcome. After all, he is *your* family. Invite Lina too, if you like. We will be one big happy family." His dark eyes twinkled as he looked down at her.

"Family," she repeated quietly. "You know, I've never had much of that before."

"You have it now." He took her hand in his. "That is, if you *want* it. If you're ready to make Montovia your home."

"It is my home," she admitted. "I think I've known that for a while."

He beamed at her. "Can we seal that with a kiss?"

She nodded eagerly. It was a done deal.

Melody Carlson is the award-winning author of more than 250 books with sales of more than 7.5 million, including many bestselling Christmas novellas, young adult titles, and contemporary romances. She received a *Romantic Times* Career Achievement Award, and her novel *All Summer Long* has been made into a Hallmark movie. The movie based on her novel *The Happy Camper* premiered on UPtv in 2023. She and her husband live in central Oregon. Learn more at www.MelodyCarlson.com.

More Christmas
Magic *Awaits*

Fall in Love
This Christmas

MEET
Melody

— MelodyCarlson.com —

f melodycarlsonauthor
⊙ authormelodycarlson